Praise for Danilo ᴋ

"*Garden, Ashes* will influence the most current trends in the art of the literary avant-garde—so much so that it may even shape the course of the novel."
—*Le Figaro*

"Kiš is one of the handful of incontestably major writers of the second half of the century. . . . His work preserves the honor of literature."
—Susan Sontag, *Partisan Review*

"An absolutely first-rate book, one of the best things I've ever seen on the whole experience of communism in Eastern Europe, but more than that, it's really a first-rate novel."
—Irving Howe

"*Garden, Ashes* is a singularly moving evocation of being a child without childhood, and of a family trying to survive the end of the world. . . . But far transcending the facts, however dramatic, is Kiš's manner of dealing with them. The potent blend of lyrical poignancy and sardonic irreverence transforms childhood and exile into an original vision of exceptional force and beauty."
—Ernst Pawel, *Nation*

Other Books by Danilo Kiš in English Translation

Early Sorrows
The Encyclopedia of the Dead
Homo Poeticus
Hourglass
A Tomb for Boris Davidovich

garden, ashes

a novel by
Danilo Kiš

Introduction by Aleksandar Hemon
Translation by William J. Hannaher

Dalkey Archive Press

Originally published in Serbo-Croatian by Prosveta as *Bašta, pepeo,* 1965
First published in English by Harcourt, Inc., 1975
English translation copyright ©1975 by Harcourt, Inc.
Introduction copyright © 2003 by Aleksandar Hemon

Published by arrangement with Harcourt, Inc.

First Dalkey Archive edition, 2003

Library of Congress Cataloging-in-Publication Data

Kiš, Danilo, 1935-1989.
    [Bašta, pepeo. English]
    Garden, ashes / Danilo Kiš ; introduction by Aleksandar Hemon ; translated by William
J. Hannaher.— 1st Dalkey Archive ed.
        p. cm.
    Originally published: New York : Harcourt Brace Jovanovich, 1975.
    ISBN 1-56478-326-X
    I. Hannaher, William J. II. Title.

PG1419.21.I8B313 2003
891.8'2354—dc21
                                                                2003055104

Partially funded by a grant from the Illinois Arts Council.

Dalkey Archive Press books are published by the Center for Book Culture, a nonprofit organization.

www.centerforbookculture.org

Printed on permanent/durable acid-free paper and bound in the United States of America.

Introduction

Let us not mince words here: Danilo Kiš's *Garden, Ashes* is an unmitigated masterpiece, surely not just one of the best books about the Holocaust, but one of the greatest books of the past century. The fact that it went out of print is a sad testimony to the current American literary situation, but now it is back in all its splendor and sorrow.

Danilo Kiš was born in 1935 (he died in 1989) of a Montenegrin mother and a Jewish father. He was born in Subotica, which was then in Yugoslavia, now in Serbia and Montenegro, a relatively prosperous town close to the Hungarian border. This fact is relevant for the understanding of *Garden, Ashes,* as Subotica fell under Hungarian control with the German attack on Yugoslavia in April 1941. The position of Hungarian Jews in the Holocaust was unique—despite an occasional pogrom (as the one in Novi Sad in 1942, to which references can be found in *Garden, Ashes,* as well as in *Hourglass* and *Psalm 44,* Kiš's other novels belonging to his "family cycle") and common anti-Semitism, the far-right regime of Admiral Horthy avoided full partici- pation in the "Final Solution" until 1944, when Horthy was replaced with the Arrow Cross, the Hungarian Nazis. The Soviet forces were rapidly advancing toward Budapest, and the Arrow Cross, with the help of the Germans, started shipping off Hungarian Jews to death camps. (Eichmann himself visited Budapest in 1944 in order to speed up the genocide.) Thus, the last trains arriving in Auschwitz consisted largely of Hungarian Jews. On one of those trains was Kiš's father.

Kiš's work is a supreme example of the tragic impossibility of separating the personal and the historical, particularly in the lives of people who cannot afford the illusion that history can be run like a profitable corporation. For Eduard Scham, the father in *Garden, Ashes,* ends up on the same train to Auschwitz as Kiš's father. One could easily, and lazily, conclude that the story of *Garden, Ashes,* the story of the tragic wanderings of the Scham family, is a concealed memoir, a confessional project intent on conveying how Kiš may have "felt" as a "victim" of the Holocaust. But what makes *Garden, Ashes* a masterpiece is that, rather than being merely personal and thus descriptive, it is profoundly transformative. That is to say, even if Kiš starts from a personal space, the experience of the Holocaust is transformed into a literary experience; it is reconstituted as simultaneously personal, historical, and literary. Of course, the Holocaust changed not only the way a person thought of himself/herself, but the way we (the survivors) think of literature—for the Holocaust was an unprecedented historical event, and nothing has ever been the same after it, particularly literature. The form and the content of *Garden, Ashes* are also transformative, continuously affecting each other until there is nothing but the organic unity of a literary experience.

If one is forced to declare what *Garden, Ashes* is about—such declaration always violating a work of art—one would have to say that it is about the relation between imagination and history, between poetry and genocide. To the well-known question of whether poetry is possible after the Holocaust, Kiš answers a resounding yes—indeed, not just possible, but inescapably necessary. But poetry/literature after the Holocaust is unavoidably transformed and transformative, because it has to use imagination to understand the unimaginable, and to do this it has to acknowledge the failure of imagination in the face of horror as enormous as the Holocaust. One has to write with humility if one is to restore the possibility of human history and humanistic literature, starting, as it were, from scratch, from the smallest things.

Thus Kiš opens *Garden, Ashes* with something small, with a tray, as though offering his enormous talent on it. The narrator's mother carries the tray, with a jar of honey and a bottle of cod-liver oil, along with "the amber hues of sunny days, thick concentrates full of intoxicating aromas." Kiš goes beyond the content, as it were, and gives us a nearly microscopic description of the *form* of the tray, with "a raised rim" along its edges and flaky patches of nickel that look like "tin foil pressed out under fingernails." There are "tiny decorative protuberances—whole chain of little metallic grapes" on the outer edge of the rim, which can be felt "like Braille letters, under the flesh of the thumb." And around those grapes "ringlike layers of grease had collected, barely visible, like shadows cast by little cupolas."

The tray is tactile—the reader touches it with Andi's mother. Kiš is never afraid to go from a small detail to an even smaller detail—from the "grapes" to their tiny shadows. The realm of the barely visible is where Kiš is most comfortable, but once he perceives it he augments it—the tray is taking up the entire screen in the mind's projection room. He achieves this by comparing the grease rings with cupola shadows—the comparison spanning from the infinitesimal to the humongous. At the same time, the emotional size of the tray is increased by upgrading the little jars and glasses to "specimens of the new lands at which the foolish barge of our days would be putting ashore."

The patience with which Kiš goes deeper into the tray, looking for a more precise detail, betokens his conviction that the exactness of the detail, as miniscule as it may be, opens doors into whole new worlds—an operation required if one is to employ imagination to comprehend history. By choosing a unique, specific detail, Kiš implies that the world and human life consist of an infinite number of details and that the writer's job is to uncover them, to expose them to the reader's eye, particularly if he's about to show that history infuses the smallest of human spaces, as there's no escape from it.

Opening a novel with a beaten-up tray loaded with details is exactly the opposite from the godlike point of view of the "great novel" openings: say, a Dickensian description of the city; or Tolstoy's great generalizations about happy and unhappy families; or Bellow's immediate invasion of Herzog's mind. Many a novel opens with a peal of self-importance, which Kiš systematically ignores. *Garden, Ashes* is determinedly *ungreat,* for how can someone who has had the experience of the Holocaust ever be deluded into feeling important, let alone great. Amazingly, that is exactly what makes *Garden, Ashes* great, even if its seeming *ungreatness* made it disappear under the radar of the American literary establishment, which produces "great" books on a weekly basis.

What is even more astonishing is that, before we're aware that the central event of *Garden, Ashes* is the Holocaust, we enter the apocalyptic stage with the tray in our hands. By insisting on the materiality of the tray, along with giving the narrative voice to a boy, Andi Scham, Kiš instantly dismisses the ambition of explaining the Holocaust, as such ambition is bound to fail ignobly. The most we can hope for is experiencing it vicariously in language, our experience admittedly limited to the barely visible, but all the more transformative and therefore true because of that.

The Holocaust is an Apocalypse, a cosmic event, and Kiš unabashedly covers the cosmic—in the sense of all-inclusive—end of human experience. Eduard Scham, Andi's father, who will disappear in Auschwitz, is a crazy prophet or a prophetic madman. He gives ranting, messianic sermons to his befuddled family, and uses a map of the sky to follow stars on his peregrinations. He works on the *Bus, Ship, Rail, and Air Travel Guide,* which at some point goes well beyond its initial ambition of answering the question: "How can we travel to Nicaragua?" It becomes a cosmological compendium, a description of the universe that is to perish with him in Auschwitz, for which he collects literature "in the most diverse disciplines, in almost all European languages." Kiš, ever a master of lists, conveys the magnitude of Eduard Scham's project by listing meticulously, in neat alphabetical order, some two hundred disciplines he explored in writing his travel guide. Once the novel is raised to a cosmic/Apocalyptic level, "the multitude of details that make up human life" (Kiš's *Encyclopedia of the Dead*) that Kiš has so patiently collected attains cosmic proportions and universal importance. The details are what the universe of *Garden, Ashes*—the universe marked by genocide—is made of. Kiš is much like the contemporary physicist who needs to study matter at subatomic levels in order to understand how space came into being, while understanding, even if unwillingly, how an apocalypse can stem from "science."

Kiš's sensibility is a materialist one. The world consists of material particles that are experienced by people in history, as transcendence went up in the air through the chimneys of Auschwitz. Hence, he employs his detail in order to enter philosophical depths, to reach ontological conclusions. This requires even more, rather than less, precision—the more abstract the thought the more it has to be pinpointed by the specificity of the detail. Here is an example. In *Garden, Ashes,* little Andi Scham suffers from insomnia, caused by the presence of death in his thoughts (and everywhere around him):

> When I thought of death, and I thought of it as soon as darkness enveloped the room, the thought unwound itself, like a roll of black silk thrown from a fourth-floor window. No matter how hard I tried the thought inexorably unwound to the end, borne along by its own weight.

Every time I read this passage I hear the fluttering of the silk—the sound of the idea of death. The idea has been materialized: the black silk roll is the objective correlative of a death thought, evanescent and evasive though it may be. But Kiš knows that to achieve this the writing has to be absolutely precise: the death silk roll has to be thrown from the *fourth* floor, not the third floor or the fifth floor. (In the Serbo-Croatian original, the roll is thrown from the third floor, but that is because what is the first floor in the U.S. is the mezzanine in Europe—the translator, to his credit, felt compelled to be just as precise as Kiš.) There is, of course, no way of knowing what the difference in the roll unwinding would be if it were thrown from the third or the fifth floor, but by refusing to leave it open to negotiation, Kiš suggests that he knows *exactly* what he is talking about—and who are we not to trust him? Clearly, we are in the hands of a master, confident in one's own experience and competence as well as the reader's intelligence—a far cry from cowardly contemporary writing, ever fretting over the impatient, lazy reader.

I have taught *Garden, Ashes* to American students. Everything was set against it: a book, barely in print at the time, by an obscure Eastern European writer, dealing with the Holocaust, to which they were trained to respond in a ready-made, clichéd way ("Never again!" plus tolerance and respect for "other cultures" as the opposite of racism, etc). On top of that, *Garden, Ashes* is a book that is easy to describe as demanding—a crippling epithet in American mainstream culture, which bends over backwards to make the consumer-citizen happy and undisturbed. But once I managed to convince them that *demanding* is not only okay, but necessary, that history, the suffering of others, the need for communicating the incommunicable must be *demanding*, they could discover the beauty of Kiš's poetry, the force of his imagination, the power of his literature. They could learn that those who find the world *undemanding* are either idiots, or backed by a vast, mindless military power, or, as is the case now, both. And my students loved it.

Let us, then, not mince words and get to the reading of *Garden, Ashes*, a masterpiece that teaches us how to face history with language.

Aleksandar Hemon
2003

garden, ashes

L ATE in the morning on summer days, my mother would come into the room softly, carrying that tray of hers. The tray was beginning to lose its thin nickelized glaze. Along the edges where its level surface bent upward slightly to form a raised rim, traces of its former splendor were still present in flaky patches of nickel that looked like tin foil pressed out under the fingernails. The narrow, flat rim ended in an oval trough that bent downward and was banged in and misshapen. Tiny decorative protuberances—a whole chain of little metallic grapes—had been impressed on the upper edge of the rim. Anyone holding the tray (usually my mother) was bound to feel at least three or four of these semicylindrical protuberances, like Braille letters, under the flesh of the thumb. Right there, around those grapes, ringlike layers of grease had collected, barely visible, like shadows cast by little cupolas. These small rings, the color of dirt under fingernails, were remnants of coffee grounds, cod-liver oil, honey, sherbet. Thin crescents on the smooth, shiny surface of the tray showed where glasses had just been removed. Without opening my eyes, I knew from the crystal tinkling of teaspoons against glasses that my mother had set down the tray for a moment and was moving toward the window, the picture of determination, to push the dark curtain aside. Then the room would come aglow in the dazzling light of the morning, and I would shut my eyes tightly as the spectrum alternated from yellow to blue to red. On her tray, with her jar of honey and her bottle of cod-liver oil, my mother carried to us the amber hues of sunny days, thick concentrates full of intoxicating aromas. The little jars and glasses were just samples, specimens of the new lands at which the foolish barge of our days would be putting ashore on those summer mornings. Fresh water glistened in the glass, and we would drink it down expertly, in tiny sips, clucking like experienced tasters. We would sometimes express dissatisfaction by grimacing and coughing: the water was tasteless, greasy like rainwater, and full of autumnal sediment, while the honey had lost its color and turned thick and turbid, showing the first signs of crystallization. On rainy days, cloudy and gloomy, our fingerprints would stay on the teaspoon handle. Then, sad and disappointed, hating to get up, we would back under the covers to sleep through a day that had started out badly.

The branches of the wild chestnut trees on our street reached out to touch each other. Vaults overgrown with ivy-like leafage thrust in between these tall arcades. On ordinary windless days, this whole architectural structure would stand motionless, solid in its daring. From time to time the sun would hurtle its futile rays through the dense leafage. Once they had penetrated the slanting, intertwined branches, these rays would quiver for a while before melting and dripping onto the Turkish cobblestones like liquid silver. We pass underneath these solemn arches, grave and deserted, and hurry down the arteries of the city. Silence is everywhere, the dignified solemnity of a holiday morning. The postmen and salesclerks are still asleep behind the closed, dusty shutters. As we move along past the low one-story houses, we glance at each other and smile, filled with respect: the wheez-

4

ings of the last sleepers are audible through the dark swaying curtains and accordion shutters. The great ships of sleep are sailing the dark Styx. At times it seems as though the engines will run down, that we are on the verge of a catastrophic failure. One engine starts to rattle, to lose its cadence, to falter, as if the ship has run aground on some underwater reef. But the damage has apparently been repaired, or possibly there had never been any damage at all. We are sailing downstream, at thirty knots. Alongside the panting sleepers stand large metal alarm clocks, propped up on their hind legs like roosters, pecking away at the fine seeds of the minutes, and then—charged to the point of an explosion, stuffed, enraged—they strain their legs against the marble surface of the night table just before beginning to crow triumphantly, to crow in swaying, bloody crests.

Lugging her cardboard boxes, Fräulein Weiss shows up on the street corner facing the caserne. Thin, gnarled legs in orange socks peer out from underneath her ragged clothing. Fräulein Weiss, an elderly German woman, sells sugar candies. As she sways along, bent under her burden, sheltered by her boxes and tied to them by a cord made of paper, only her head peeps out, as though she were carrying her own head in a box under her arm. Age and illness have transformed her face into a dark puddle. Wrinkles have spread radially from her mouth, which, like the wound in Christ's palm, has shifted to the center of her face. All the channels of her wrinkles flow, starlike, into that one place, that huge old wound. You see, children, this heap of eroded bones, this shuffling, this rattling—is a whole brilliant, kitschy novel, the last chapter in a threadbare volume, replete with splendor, festivities, defeats. One of the survivors of the spectacular sinking of the *Titanic*, Fräulein Weiss had once attempted suicide. Imitating some famous actress, she had filled up her hotel room with roses. All day the bellhops and elevator boys were delivering bouquets of the most fragrant flowers, like cherubs. The elevators that day turned into great hanging gardens, into greenhouses that carried the burden of their fragrances up into heaven and then came back down again at a dizzying pace, their orientation all gone. Thousands of pink carnations, hyacinths, lilacs, irises, hundreds of white lilies, all had to be sacrificed. But her soul, lulled by the fragrances and intermixed with them, would soar up somewhere, hovering above, relieved of one life, on into the rose gardens of paradise, or would turn into a flower, into an iris. . . . The next day, she was found unconscious amidst the murderous flowers. Subsequently, as the victim of the vengeance of the flower gods, she fell beneath automobiles and streetcars. Peasant carts and swift fiacres ran over her. Yet every time she emerged from under the wheels hurt but alive. Thus, in her passionate brush with death, she had come to know the secret of everlasting life. Groaning and emitting painful sounds from her depths, like a child crying, she passes by us like the filthy, yellowed pages of some worn novel. . . . *Gut'n Morgen, Fräulein Weiss, küss die Hand!*

A little further on, local Germans wearing lederhosen and carrying knapsacks on their backs are starting out on a weekend excursion. Golden mallets quiver on their muscular legs. Inside their belts, they carry magnificent scouting knives with rosewood handles. They are playing harmonicas, mimicking crickets. In front of the pastry shop at the corner, they pop open bottles of pink soda that smells like eau de cologne. Then they return the harmonicas to their fishy mouths and bite down, dividing their instruments into three parts with single thrusts of their powerful jaws. Small streetcars, blue, yellow, and green, are racing to catch up with each other in their senseless cruising through the deserted holiday streets, sounding melodious tunes on their lyres and tinkling their bells gently.

We arrive shortly at a small red train which transports swimmers in the summertime and which in the off season dashes about the woods and fields entirely according to its own mood and disposition. The miniature train, with its pretty little locomotive, looks like a rope chain of red bugs. The cars of the train shove and smash against each other, an outsized raspberry-colored accordion playing dance tunes. Then this dragonfly, this carnival enticement, begins to fly away, buzzing and puffing along, and the poppies in the grainfields beside the track draw long unbroken lines as though inscribed with a red pencil.

My dizziness grows more and more unbearable, and my mother takes me by the hand. By the time we reach the castle, I am squinting. All I can remember is the fireworks display flaring up in front of my tightly closed eyes. I move forward blindly, guided by my mother's hand, my shoulders occasionally grazing against a tree trunk.

We stand by the castle fence, pushing our hands through the bars. First a doe and then a stag, with their great dark eyes. Springing from the dense underbrush, from hidden, enigmatic corners of the Count's forest, they come out of their dignified captivity, proud in their bearing and gait, a bit on the blasé side. On their supple legs, with dark moist spots on their noses, they approach the fence to take sugar cubes from my mother's hands.

Borne along by the inertia of our days and by habit, we continued to visit the castle all through that summer. Since the castle had obviously been abandoned, we appropriated it for ourselves without benefit of the law. My mother would not only say "our deer" but "our castle," even though we had never passed beyond the fence to encroach on the castle's solitude and dignity. We simply believed, and I completely agree with my mother on this point, that we had every right to consider an abandoned castle—offering the beauty of its ruins to the inquisitive eye—to be part of our own resources, that we could lay claim to it accordingly, just as we laid claim to the golden hull of that sun-filled day. Presuming this discovery to be due at least in part to our own merits, we decided to keep it a secret, to tell no one where we were spending our weekends.

Then came the last days of summer, a half season, half summer and half autumn. In the morning the air allowed the assumption that summer was still in its prime and that the blush on the leaves was the consequence of a long heat wave. The chestnut trees in front of the house, long since deprived of their fruits, were shedding in their lazy way. The leaves, yellow and smelling like tobacco, had started to fall indecisively from the branches. My mother decided that we should have confidence in the color of the sky—various shades of aquamarine—and in the promise of the morning sun. While we were standing on the bridge my mother had a peculiar presentiment about the advent of autumn. Indeed, the waters of the Danube were strangely altered, a muddy green, full of some dubious sediment that meant showers somewhere in Switzerland. The hints in the air of rain made us head straight for the red train, even though there was not a cloud in the sky. Our decision was a wise one, no doubt about it. We climbed aboard the last train of the summer season, decorated for the occasion with strips of crepe paper and wild flowers. A gentleman wearing a bowler, presumably representing the provincial government, gave a speech that my mother considered amusing and affecting. "Gentlemen," he intoned, "in honor of this last train of the summer season, and to the greater glory of our town's traditions, the red train today—on its last trip of the season—is going to take all passengers . . . all passengers . . ." Applause and shouts of "Long live the orator," along with the happy yells of children, drowned out his concluding words, since the word had been going around town that the traditional ceremony would be canceled due to certain events in the realm of foreign policy that favored economy and caution in daily affairs.

My mother's suspicions had proved correct. We had just reached the castle when darkness, looming over the hills of Fruška Gora, began to spread toward us. We did not even have time to coax the doe and stag over to us. The dark cloud was upon us, and rain began to patter down.

To protect ourselves from the rain, we took a short cut through the woods. We emerged completely soaked and intoxicated with ozone. All at once, we realized that we were lost. In vain did my mother attempt to hide the fact from us. The rain had totally altered the appearance of the area. . . .

My mother crossed herself, stopping abruptly. A herd of black buffalo charged out of the woods, thundering like a regiment of cavalry, veiled in mist, suicidally resolved to resist the onslaught of the water, to silence the ironic chorus of the frogs. In close formation, horns in attack position, the buffalo were leaping out of the woods, marching fearlessly with a Prussian step toward the swamps. At that very instant, the rain stopped, and we succeeded—at the last moment—in reaching the main road. From where we stood we could see the buffalo vanishing into the muddy quicksand, a cleverly prepared trap. They sank helplessly and fast.

My mother, affected by the gruesome sight and aware of the danger we had eluded, crossed herself once more. . . .

When we returned to town, signs of autumn's offensive were everywhere. Huge yellow posters called for order and compliance on the part of the citizenry, and an airplane was dropping leaflets—yellow and red—speaking in the arrogant language of the victor about the forthcoming reprisal.

"Your uncle is dead," my mother said. The tinkling of silver teaspoon against crystal was louder, betraying the trembling of her hands, and I opened my eyes to check my suspicion. She looked pale in the glare of the sunlight, as if her face were powdered. Her eyes were framed by pink circles. Sensing my confusion, she whispered, without looking at me, "You didn't know him." She seemed surprised and touched by the fact that this sudden death had frustrated an acquaintance full of promise. Following the train of her own thoughts, or perhaps mine, she added, "And now you will never see him." The word "death," the divine seed that my mother sowed in my curiosity that morning, began to soak up all the fluids coursing through my consciousness. The consequences of this premature gestation turned palpable all too fast: dizziness and nausea. My mother's words, while entirely obscure, suggested to me that some dangerous idea lurked behind them. With my mother's approval, I set out, with head bowed, to get a breath of fresh air. Actually it was just an attempt to escape. I went out in front of the house and leaned against a wall. I looked at the sky through the bare branches of the wild chestnut tree. The day was ordinary, routine. And then, all of a sudden, I sensed some strange anxiety in my intestines, some torment and agitation hitherto unknown to me, as though castor oil were rampaging around my stomach. I was looking through half-open eyes at the sky, like the first man, and thinking about how—there you are—my uncle had died, about how they would now be burying him, about how I would never meet him. I stood petrified, thinking that one day I too would die. At the same time I was horror-stricken to realize that my mother would also die. All of this came rush-

ing upon me in a flash of a peculiar violet color, in a twinkling, and the sudden activity in my intestines and in my
heart told me that what had seemed at first just a foreboding
was indeed the truth. This experience made me realize,
without any circumlocution, that I would die one day, and
so would my mother, and my sister Anna. I couldn't imagine
how one day my hand would die, how my eyes would die.
Looking over my hand, I caught this thought on my palm,
connected to my body, indivisible from it. Astonished and
frightened, I had suddenly come to understand that I was a
boy by the name of Andreas Scham, called Andi by my
mother, that I was the only one with that particular name,
with that nose, with that taste of honey and cod-liver oil in
his mouth, the only one in the world whose uncle had died
of tuberculosis the previous day, the only boy who had a sister
named Anna and a father named Eduard Scham, the only
one in the world who was thinking at that particular moment
that he was the only boy named Andreas Scham, whom his
mother called by the pet name Andi. The flow of my thoughts
reminded me of a tube of toothpaste that my sister had
bought a few days earlier, on which there was a picture of
a young lady smiling and holding a tube on which a young
lady was smiling and holding a tube. . . . The mirror game
tormented and exhausted me, because it did not let my
thoughts come to a halt on their own—on the contrary, it
crumbled them still more, turning them into a fine powder
that hung in the air, in which there was a picture of a young
lady smiling and holding in her hand a tube on which . . . a
young lady, oh yes, a young lady . . .

At first it was easier for me to bear the thought of my
own death—in which I simply did not wish to believe—than
the thought of my mother's. At the same time, I became
aware that I would not be in attendance at my own death,
just as I was not in attendance at my dreaming, and that

calmed me down a bit. Moreover, I started to believe in my own immortality. I thought that since I already knew the secret of death, that is to say, since I was aware of the existence of death (I called it "the secret of death" in my own mind), I had thereby discovered the secret of immortality. With this belief in hand, this illusion of my own omnipotence, I succeeded in calming myself down, and I no longer felt the fear of dying so much as some kind of tearful melancholy over the death of my mother. Despite everything, I was not so irrational as to believe that I would succeed in sparing her and my other relatives from death. I kept this right for myself alone, not out of selfishness but out of an awareness that I would not be in a position to come up with so much trickery as that—there would scarcely be room for myself.

I couldn't fall asleep that night. This was the start of the nightmare that tormented me all through my childhood. Since the thought of death particularly obsessed me in the evening, just before bedtime, I began to fear going to bed: I was afraid of being alone in the room. My mother, realizing from the raving and screaming I did in my sleep that I was overcome by some childish fright, gave in and let me be lulled to sleep by the velvety voice of the epileptic Miss Edith. I was to start school the following year, so everyone made fun of me for my attachment to my mother, and so did Miss Edith, who, by her own admission, was in love with me. But my mother was pleased by my devotion and always took my side, saying that I was excessively sensitive, which she liked, since it proved that I would not be selfish like my father, although at the same time it made her worry a lot about my future. By the time the guests departed, I had long since fallen asleep, having forgotten for a moment to think about my mission, about how I was going to outwit death, about how I would one day have to be in attendance at my mother's death. She would be lying in a bed of flowers, just as Madame

Melanie had the previous year, and I would uselessly call out her name and kiss her. Afterward, they would take her away to the cemetery and bury her under beds of roses. . . . Though I tried very hard, I was never able to bring this thought to its conclusion. And yet my nightmares were an effort to avoid bringing this thought to its conclusion. When I thought of death, and I thought of it as soon as darkness enveloped the room, the thought unwound itself, like a roll of black silk thrown from a fourth-floor window. No matter how hard I tried, the thought inexorably unwound to the end, borne along by its own weight. . . .

First I knelt down in my blue pajamas next to my sister Anna and whispered a prayer to God, staring up at a painting of an angel watching over children as they cross a bridge. It was a cheap lithograph in color, in a narrow gilt frame, that my mother had received when Anna was born. A little girl with a bouquet of wild flowers in her hand is crossing the bridge, along with a little boy in short pants. The bridge is rotting; planks have fallen off. Under the bridge, down below in the abyss, a foaming stream rumbles away. Evening is descending, a thunderstorm looms on the horizon. The little girl is holding on to her straw hat, while the little boy hangs on to the twisted railing of the bridge. And above them, above their insecure steps, above the violet gloom, hovers the guardian angel with its wings extended, the nymph of children's dreams, butterfly-woman, *Chrysidia Bellona*. Only the toes of its divine feet show underneath its pink tunic, while the arc of its wings ends in a tip of fiery brilliance. My mother used to say that my sister and I were that little girl and boy, and for a long time I believed that we truly were, fixed at a moment when we were wandering through that area and our guardian angel was not on the alert. So I was looking, then, at the painting of the angel hanging over our bed and was praying quietly. But once I had finished the "Our Father"

13

and another prayer that my mother had carefully composed, which I no longer remember, I would lie down and pull the blanket all the way over my head and begin praying for a long life for my mother and my nearest relatives. Then, since this prayer amounted essentially to thinking of death, I would begin to shudder from fear and from the strain of trying not to think about it, because fatigue would overcome me gradually. I would begin counting to keep the black silk from falling abruptly, to avoid thinking, to prevent my own thought from unwinding to the end. One night, when I was weakened by fatigue, however, a diabolical idea came to me. I had counted up to sixty (I knew how to count to two hundred) when that number ceased to figure in my consciousness as just a prime number devoid of any sense other than as part of a child's telling his beads to lull himself to sleep—we may similarly pronounce a given word countless times, over and over again, straining to discern through the name the word's meaning, the object denominated by the word, yet then at one instant it is exactly the substance of the word that is spilled out like a liquid, leaving only the word's empty crystal dish. Instead, through a contrary process, one of the numbers had become a beaker. At the bottom of the beaker, the dark sediment of meaning was sloshing about. One of the numbers had become at that instant *a number of years*, and thereby all the remaining numbers had taken on the same significance: the number of years left in my mother's life. What sort of a lifetime is that, two hundred years, for the mother of a boy who is resolved to elude death's grasp, not like a lizard but as a person who has, who will have, a sure plan (no room for chance or improvising there), a plan to be conceived and developed through a whole human lifetime? So I counted to two hundred, and back again. My awareness that you could count all your life and never come to the final number, as Anna said, since the last number would always be followed

14

by the next one, only brought the nearness and certainty of my mother's death closer to my eyes. The numbers were years, and I knew—by a rough mathematical reckoning that same night—that my mother could not live more than another seventy or eighty years, since she was over thirty-five, and the oldest of old people, somewhere in Russia (so said Mr. Gavanski), lived barely one hundred and twenty years. Tormented by this counting, I suddenly got lost in eternity's abyss, and the last consolation that I would not founder down below against some underwater reef was the hand of my mother, whose presence I verified with the last atom of my tortured consciousness. . . .

My mother told me one evening, after kissing me good night and turning on the night light, that in a few days we would be starting off on a train trip. She was fully aware of the effect her words would have on me—she knew that my thinking about the trip would utterly upset me, tire me out like our children's games, that I would soon fall asleep, lulled in advance by the clatter of the wheels of the train and by the churning of the locomotive. Afterward, half-asleep, I heard my mother coming slowly into the room and whispering, since she must have seen that I had not yet dozed off, "Imagine you're *already* traveling." All of a sudden, my bed, my mother and I, the flower vase, the marble-topped nightstand and the glass of water, my father's cigarettes, the angel that watches over children, my mother's Singer sewing machine, the night lamp, the dressers and curtains, the whole room started traveling through the night like a first-class railway carriage, and this compelling illusion put me to sleep as depots and towns passed alongside me in my dreams, with names that my father would roll over his tongue in a fever, raving. For my father was working at that time on the third or fourth edition of one of his most poetic books: the then-famous *Bus, Ship, Rail, and Air Travel Guide.* Veiled in the blue smoke of his cigarette, red-eyed, irritable, slightly intoxicated, this genius of travel, this Wandering Jew looked like a poet being consumed by the fire of creative inspiration.

I come to slowly in the morning, still not knowing where I am, who I am, what my name is, I am awakening as birds do, as lizards do. All at once, though, through an immense anticipation or through some childish music that penetrates my consciousness and hovers in the room, I recall my mother's words of the previous evening. Making no effort to open my eyes, I give myself over completely to this enthusiasm. Then I hear Anna sloshing her tongue about, turning over in her mouth the last moist morsels of the bread of dreams. My eyes are half-open as I tell her, "We're starting out on a trip tomorrow." I want her to confirm my words, I want to persuade myself that I have not dreamed it all up. But before Anna has time to tell me that she knew it before I did, that Mama had told her long ago, that they just wanted to avoid telling me earlier so that I wouldn't get too excited and bother them with my questions, I hear my mother turning the poppy-seed mill, and I pick up the odor of vanilla and poppy seeds coming from the kitchen, and I no longer doubt that we will be traveling. Poppy-seed cakes mean travel, there can be no doubt about it. So I jump out of bed and run to the kitchen to help my mother scrape up filling from the bottom of the pot. The day passes in a festive fever. Anna wraps boiled eggs in paper napkins, our yellow pigskin suitcase lies on the table. The smell of tanned leather and glue wafts up, and the dark-yellow silken lining is reflected in bright shades on the inside of the lid: odor of mint, mothballs, and eau de cologne.

Our things are packed and standing on the table. The suitcase is tied with straps. The traveling bag and the thermos are alongside it. The smell of the poppy-seed cakes fills the room: from them comes their soul, comprising powders of exotic plants, vanilla, cinnamon, and poppy seeds. By their luxurious demise, these spices testify to the ritual exaltation of travel, to which they are to be sacrificed, like incense.

In the evening, when we go to bed, my father smokes in the dark. I see floating around his head the burning firefly, the radiant winged insect of his genius. I am sure that I will not be able to fall asleep that night. I have been lying awake so long that it seems to me that dawn should already be at hand, so I lift my head to hear if the others are asleep or are just pretending, but then I sense that my head is drooping from tiredness and that I will not really be meeting the dawn awake. Yet there is no way for me to comprehend how sleep comes on all at once, without any effort of will or knowledge on my part, how I can fall asleep every night without catching hold of that instant when the angel of sleep, that great butterfly of night, swoops down to close my eyes with its wings. So I begin to set an ambush for that instant. I would have liked to catch hold of sleep at least once, just as I had been resolved to catch hold of death one day, to catch hold of the wings of the angel of sleep when it came for me, to grab it with two fingers like a butterfly after sneaking up on it from behind. I use precisely this metaphor because when I say "the angel of sleep" I am thinking—just as I was when I believed in the angel of sleep—of the moment when the waking state passes into the state of oblivion, for I long believed —and I think I was right—that this shift occurs all of a sudden, for—if the organism lulls itself to sleep over a long interval— consciousness has to sink all at once, like a stone. And yet I wanted to catch the angel of sleep in its insidious fortress, so I let myself be lulled, I even tried with all my strength to lull myself to sleep, and then I would jerk my head at the last moment, when I thought that I was catching myself *sinking into sleep*. But I was never wholly satisfied with this torturous experiment. Sometimes I woke up ten times in a row, with the last effort of my consciousness, the supreme force of will of the one who was going to outwit death someday. My sleep game was practice for the grand struggle with death. But it always seemed to me to be not the right moment, it seemed that I had made rash moves, because I never succeeded in getting so much as a peek into sleep, and my intention had been exactly that. Instead, once I had roused myself before the very gates of sleep, the angel would have taken flight, would have hidden somewhere behind my head, in some mousehole, who knows where. On one occasion, though, I seemed to have caught sleep in the act, *in flagrante delicto* as it were. I was saying to myself, thinking to myself: "I am awake, I am awake." I lay there waiting with this thought as though in an ambush, waiting for someone—the angel of sleep or God—to dispute my thought, to come and deny my thought and prevent me from thinking it. I would have wanted to verify who the angel of sleep was and how it was capable of halting all at once the flow of my thoughts—this one simple sentence, to be exact, this bare thought that I did not want to surrender without a struggle. At that point, tormented by the strain of avoiding the surrender of this thought, and in the absence of the angel of sleep (who failed to come to dispute me and must have been aware of the fact that I was observing), I resorted to a trick: I would cease to think that thought so as to make the angel believe that I had decided, incautious and overcome by fatigue, to surrender without resistance, to close my eyes. Yet it was not easy to stop thinking this simple thought of mine—"I am awake"—all at once, for this thought had broken off on its own, carried along by inertia. The harder I tried not to think it, the more obtrusive it became, just as when I tried not to hear the ticking of the alarm clock on the nightstand I became more clearly aware of its tick-tock, tick-tock than ever. And when I finally succeeded in forgetting this thought, really and truly, I would sink into sleep without knowing how it had happened, just as I succeeded in not hearing the ticking of the clock only when I was not thinking about it or when I was already asleep. Nonetheless, once or twice, as I was saying, I actually succeeded in rousing myself at precisely the moment when the wings had covered my eyes like a shadow and when I was suddenly struck by some intoxicating whiff: I had awakened from real sleep at the instant when the angel of sleep had come to take me away, yet I saw nothing, found out nothing. I finally understood that the presence of my consciousness and the presence of the angel of sleep were mutually exclusive, but I continued playing this tiring and dangerous game for a long time. I was going to hide, so when the bear Death came to sniff me out, he would be sure that I was already gone.

Suddenly the sharp buzz of the alarm clock seared into my consciousness like an unexpected flash of light, and I found myself entirely drained and defeated. Although I was aware immediately that the clock had sung out to announce the triumphal hour of the long-awaited trip, I lay with my head covered because of fatigue and because of the vengeance of the angel of sleep, whom I had wanted to grab by the wings. At first, I didn't even want to wake up or travel. The inner languor that I sensed in my body and in my consciousness, as if submerged in some warm, fragrant fluid, seemed irreplaceable to me. "Andi, Andi, it's time." I hear my mother's voice. "Have you forgotten? We're starting out today." I gradually come to and, with my eyes still closed, let her take off my pajamas and moisten my forehead. While she combs my hair, my head droops onto her shoulder.

But my drowsiness vanishes as soon as I have downed a

warm cup of coffee and caught sight of the fiacre in front of the door, dark violet in the light of the moon and the breaking dawn, a grand ship of a fiacre. The night is fresh, and the horses smell of hay and lilacs. In the light of the lantern on the fiacre, I see underneath the horses fresh yellow dung, steaming. I sit down between my mother and Anna on the back seat below the black leather top. My father sits along-side the coachman in front. Our large yellow pigskin suitcase lies before us, and our legs are wrapped in a rough camel's-hair blanket that smells of horses and urine. My mother asks a question: "Do you suppose we've forgotten anything?" My sister answers: "I have the thermos." My mother looks up at the sky and crosses herself, saying "I don't think we've for-gotten anything." Her satisfaction shows on her face: a full moon is shining, and my mother was a devotee of the new moon.

The asphalt is glistening from being washed down or rained upon, and the fiacre sails quietly on, gently rocked by the waves of the oncoming tide of dawn. Only the monotonous clatter of the ship's engine, where eight powerful pistons are churning away, is audible. I am no longer drowsy, but the fresh morning chill whiffs gently around my nose, so I hug my mother more tightly. At the depot, my father pays the coach-man and hands our baggage to the porter. Then we step up into the train, into a first-class compartment where the cobalt light of the acetylene lamps is glittering, and sit down on green plush seats from which miniature thick English grass is sprouting. Above the seats, as in a garden, is a hedge of white roses made of lace. I sit down by the window, in the place of honor. The compartment is warm, and I begin to thaw out. Flowers in green baskets rock gently in the depot, moss peering out of them. Two abbesses, looking like two big pen-guins, emerge from the semidarkness of the service entrance.

Then, all at once, the depot is on the move, so are the flowers in the swaying baskets. I look up: the white morning star, the benign star of our travels, is also on the move.

Although I had looked forward to the sight of the chestnut trees in front of the house, our room and our things, the smell of our bed linens and our house, it was nonetheless hard for me when I realized that our trip was coming to an end. Even then, like my father, I was in love with trains. The names of cities that my father uttered in his sleep, raving, had poisoned me with longing. I had become intoxicated by the music of travel, sounded by the train wheels and inscribed by swallows and migratory fowl in closely bunched trios on the telephone-wire notation system, in ad-lib performances and improvisations in between three-quarter pauses interrupted—suddenly and noisily—by the great organs of bridges and by the flute-siren that drills through distances and through the thick darkness of the night with its tired sighs and moans. I also delighted in the games of Chinese dominoes and, my nose glued to the windowpane, in the view from the train, in the dark rectangles of plowed earth, in the green rhombuses of meadowland and yellow squares of grain that fluttered—inflamed and sickly—in the blazing heat of the noonday sun. I was particularly excited by the fact, vaguely sensed, that while I was asleep my body, stretched out in the soft wing of sleep, was passing through spaces and distances despite my immobility and despite my sleeping state, and at such moments I did not fear sleep, I even felt that the exciting speed with which my body was hurtling through space and time was liberating me from death, that this speed and movement represented a triumph over death and over time. Everything—the festive nervousness of my parents' preparations for the trip, the green plush and lace in the train compartment, the light bulb the color of blue ink that my father turned on before we were to go to sleep, the aquamarine depths of that light—turned travel into some sort of quiet celebration, so that I always felt downcast on returning from a trip and, sitting half-asleep in the fiacre, I would continue to hear the wailing of the siren in the night and the melodious clacking of the train wheels. And while I was moping under the leather top of the fiacre, tired, longing for true sleep, while the coachman was waving his whip and the horses broke wind, my sister Anna cried quietly. While by no means sensitive, as our mother would say, Anna was nevertheless capable of crying at certain rare moments: after a holiday, after a trip. And if you were to ask her why she was crying, she would think it over for a minute and then tell you that she was very, very sorry that the holiday (or the trip) was over, she would smile at your astonishment and incredulity, and then she would revert to sobbing inconsolably.

I glance back at the fiacre and at the horses trotting away from the house, and I hear my mother unlocking the door. I enter, my eyes drooping from sleep and fatigue. I sense the smell of our room. It is a smell that I had forgotten but that all of a sudden reminds me that I am in our room, the smell to which I had become so accustomed that I recognized it only on returning home from a trip. It is the smell of coffee, cod-liver oil, vanilla, poppy seeds, and my father's cigarettes. It is all in a state of gentle decay, like water that has stood in a vase all night.

My mother flips the light switch. The checkered oilcloth glistens on the table, and I reach to touch it: still a little slippery from grease, and the cuts here and there darkened by now, looking like healed scars. The moisture on the ceiling has given form to a giant who has become our good spirit, the guardian of our house: full-bearded like the prophets of the Hebrews, he holds in his right hand the tablets, in his left our lamp with porcelain shade that resembles an upside-down spittoon—a comparison taken literally by flies.

"Oh," Anna says, "our room!" We glanced around our forgotten room, rediscovering its furnishings, which seemed to have grown darker in our absence. Two beds, old-fashioned, made of wood. Two dressers, in which worms had drilled tiny holes and from which a fine pink dust poured, soft and fragrant as a face powder. Marble-topped night tables beside the beds, like the tombstones of children of good family. In the corner, to the right of the door, a couch upholstered in threadbare homespun the color of rotten cherries, a fine old-fashioned couch resembling an upright piano. In the evening, or whenever it was quiet, the springs would burst into song. Above the couch, a lithograph in color: the Mona Lisa. My mother had cut it out of some magazine when the painting was involved in an outrageous theft from the Louvre or was being triumphantly returned, I can't recall which. It had been pressed under glass and inserted in a narrow gilt wooden frame. So, too, the angel that watches over children, the butterfly-woman, *Chrysidia Bellona* (the name of a butterfly in my album), before which we prayed as before an icon. The table was covered with a Hungarian lace cloth. A vase of fake blue crystal and a round metal ashtray stood on it. Another ashtray, a big green enamel one that was scratched in two or three places, rested on the marble-topped night table by my father's bed. Three transverse incisions on which cigarettes rested divided the ashtray's wide rim into three arcs of equal size. Each arc had the word "Symphonia" printed in large black letters three times, like an echo. The floor was made of good planks and squeaked very gently, like new shoes. To the right of the door, by the window, stood my mother's sewing machine—a powerful structure of cast iron resembling the arches of railroad bridges. The arches terminate at the bottom in little black wheels, also made of cast iron. The treadle is made of delicate plaited metal. The treadle is connected to the flywheel by a two-pronged joint. A cylindrical transmission belt, joined by two wire clasps, fits into the grooves of the flywheel. Another grooved wheel, much smaller than the flywheel, sits on top of the machine, next to the shiny transmission wheel, with its short radial spokes. The top of the machine, a big black elbow, is coated with lacquer. On the left, amidst the complicated mechanism of the needle and the invisible spools, the machine terminates in two cylindrical axles, like the horn of a snail. When the machine is on, the invisible spools work like silkworms spinning the thread. Inside, the name "Singer" is incised in large letters. Where the sides widen, the company emblems appear symmetrically, cast as gigantic spiders. On more careful analysis, however, we discover—not without astonishment—that the spiders plaited into the eyelets of the iron sides are not really spiders at all but rather a mechanical shuttle—magnified a hundredfold— with a spool from which the thread unwinds, as thick as a cord, magnified and therefore difficult to recognize, like the

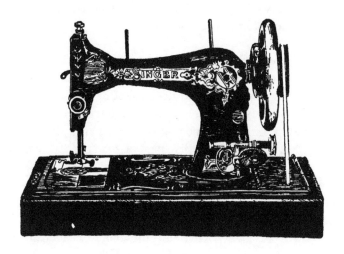

letter S, giving the illusion of spider legs. The emblem is painted a golden yellow, like a nobleman's coat of arms, and so are the arabesques on the lacquered head of the machine. They are peeling here and there and the gilt drops off in thin, delicate flakes. The wooden base has also begun to peel, especially along the edges. First it blisters from temperature changes and dampness, then it begins to wrinkle and split like diseased fingernails. A small brass emblem, elliptical like a medallion, yellow and shiny, is attached to the slender neck of the machine with two toothed screws. The same spider-spool is on the emblem, but much clearer because of its reduced dimensions. The words "The Singer Manfg. Co.—Trade Mark" appear in bas-relief on all sides, as though the machine were a coin. When I pressed the treadle, the machine hummed like a lyre. Once I broke the needle, so my mother removed the belt. But that is irrelevant now. When we came home, my gaze fell on the sewing machine before I dozed off. Because of the long train trip, presumably, and because of all the sounds that had accumulated in my ear, the machine seemed to me to be working. I could hear the wheels buzzing along and the axles sliding softly, softly.

Every now and then, in the evening, Miss Edith would come by. Her personality was linked in my mind with only the strangest of pastimes and the noblest of preoccupations, so I regarded the white hats that she brought to our home—along with a form for fashioning them—as part of her extravagance, part of her personality, part of her fate. To me, these were all Miss Edith's wedding hats. "What do you think, Mrs. Scham, about this wedding hat?" As she asked my mother the question, she would be fixing the hat and holding her melancholy head to one side. I knew her story, and this made her personality seem all the more wonderful. Miss

Edith had been engaged to a Hungarian count, who abandoned her on the very eve of the wedding. Instead of a wedding gift, he had sent her a package, a large box marked with the name of a famous eau de cologne, Chat Noir, in gilt letters. When Miss Edith opened the box, a black cat jumped out, or else it was a black cat that had been strangled with a wire, I no longer remember which. After that experience, Miss Edith became an epileptic. Since her problems were especially pronounced in the evening, when loneliness bore down on her most heavily, she had settled upon our house by virtue of the friendship between her father and mine—the loud amusements of the town cast her into a profound melancholy. Her epileptic attacks would sometimes seize her at our place, at a moment when any lyrical outburst would be least expected from her: between two quite commonplace words, or at the heart of the very silence that she had magically woven around us.

Miss Edith is creating a new wedding hat now, scooping laces and ribbons out of her bag as though removing the innards of a slaughtered chicken. My mother is observing the scene with a kind of fake indifference, while Anna is enthusiastic. From my mother's lap, I stare at Miss Edith's fingers, remembering—as though it had happened long, long ago—how she had just recently caressed me with those wonderful fingers, the fingers so splendidly equipped to handle the lace. Her long polished nails sputter when they touch the silk. She had just murmured a sentence—her voice became lower and more sublime as night came on—and the magic charms of her personality had cast a profound spell on us. When she fainted for the first time, I believed—despite my fright—that what had happened was altogether natural and that it was only by chance that Miss Edith had fainted, that the same thing might happen to any of us, especially me. I had not grasped, at that first moment, that the enchantment hovering in the air, the magnetic air enfolding us, came straight from her, from her personality, from her fingers, from the chaotic entanglement of her laces. Her eyes were big and dark, framed by barely perceptible violet circles that made her eyes seem deeper. Those eyes reflected the turbid impulses of her femininity, which she had confined, after her shocking experience, to her body's frail cocoon. Conscious of the disruptive, destructive force of her being and her sex, she had endeavored to frustrate her blood. That must have been the source of the magnetic, fragrant aroma in which she had enfolded us and from which the air took on the weight of Zeus's golden rain.

Miss Edith would fall on her back onto our red couch, where the vengeance of the gods would overtake her.

In the meantime, I would be trembling, not so much out of fear as out of some vague awareness that I was in attendance at some mysterious and extraordinary phenomenon. Miss Edith would collapse on her back without letting go of the lace. She would lift her legs, enabling me to see into the silken interior of her body. What surprised and bewildered me most at that point was the absence of the seams and stray threads that I had expected to see in this elongated ballroom glove, which is all that her body was at that moment. Instead, it was lined with silk and decorated with lace, perhaps even more luxuriantly than the facing. She would struggle desperately for a few moments, clutching her breasts, jerking and swaying her head, giving her hair its freedom as the clasps and hairpins fell out. A lascivious spasm then surges through her body. My mother immediately judges where the pressure is the strongest and unbuttons her blouse. The last thing I see is the blinding whiteness of her breasts gushing out of her blouse with a spurt. Then the sour odor of the vinegar that my mother rubs on her temples would pervade the room. Relief would follow right away. By the time I reopen my eyes, which shame had closed tight, Miss Edith would already be lying down on our couch, covered with a blanket, breathing peacefully like a child, with her arms over her head.

Miss Edith regains consciousness the way flowers open up. She opens her hairpins with her teeth and puts them back into her hair. Then she places her laces and ribbons in her bag, the hat and form in a cardboard box. No one says a word. She looks at her hands with astonishment and then buttons the single button that my mother had undone. Some strange, fragrant jumble remains behind her in the room, giving me a headache.

Miss Edith had carried into our house, into our petrified patriarchal landscape, the dark and dense fragrances of her femininity, a sort of sophisticated, dignified—noble, I should say—atmosphere. The sophisticated spleen was in her voice, in her polished nails the color of mother-of-pearl, in her neurasthenic, trembling gestures, in her paleness, in her upper-class sickness that was triggered by celebrations and enthusiasms, like the strange, seductive symbol of the black cat and the perfume of the same name written in gilt letters on the cardboard box of her enthusiasms. She injected into my dreams a sense of unease, fluid and enigmatic like the swaying of her laces, like her fragrances that brought my curiosity and my childish tranquillity into temptation. Those fragrances testified by their intoxicating presence to some other world, beyond the confines of our house, outside the boundaries of my awareness, out of reach of our comfortable routine.

Miss Edith, with her fragrances, undoubtedly artificial, caused havoc in my soul.

In the spectrum of those fragrances, only violet was the fragrance of her complexion, whereas the others, refracted through the prism of her femininity, were of unknown but presumably exotic origin and blue-blooded. From the evening when she fainted on our couch and I looked at the silk and lace in the inflamed focus of my inquisitiveness, I began to move away from my mother's lap, where I had heretofore been sitting peacefully, protected from sin and vice. From that evening on, in contrast, I preferred to sit on our couch, the color of rotten cherries, the same couch that had been the golden rain's bed and witness. It was not that my love for my mother had weakened; by no means. But my love had undergone a profound crisis: I could not find in that love an explanation for my traumas or for the shivering that would overcome me just before evening, at the time when Miss Edith's arrival—real or imagined—would burden the air with dense fragrance, the forerunner of her body. After a fictitious knock on our door, I would descend from my mother's lap and move over—ostensibly by chance—to lie down on the couch. I did not wish to deceive my mother, nor on the other hand did I want Miss Edith to find me in this state, given over to another woman's love without any reservations.

This little story might very well end here, with this shameful admission. I need not mention, I think, that my mother took note of my unfaithfulness and told me one day with pained astonishment: "I know, dear, you will leave me forever some day. You'll put me away somewhere in the attic or in the old people's home." Whereupon I began to swear to her with horrified repentance that this would never happen, and I cursed—in my mind—the moment Miss Edith had entered our house. But my mother, deeply offended by my disloyalty and bewildered by this premature deviation of my instincts, continued to torment me, to talk about her age and about her death as though it were a matter which she no longer doubted and which had only been speeded up by my action. I then began to sob, to implore her to stop talking, to take back her words, I swore my faithfulness to her without doubting for an instant my oath—I even felt a joyous kind of satisfaction at the opportunity to prove someday the truthfulness of my pledges.

Just one more thing; this is the real end of the story. My mother decided to take advantage of the first sunny day of the year, a day in spring, and do a thorough house cleaning. She opened the windows wide and Miss Edith soared out like a fragrant cloud. My mother, who had unquestionably noticed the departure, said nothing, even pretended not to have noticed anything. With two fingers, and not without veneration, she lifted a piece of lace that had fallen behind the couch and was encrusted with dust, like silver filigree. When she placed this reliquary of reliquaries in the dustpan, the lace curled into a circle like a crown. I was able to catch a last look as it lay glistening in the gold of the morning sun, piled splendidly atop the swaying fluffiness of the dust, crumpled newspapers, and broken eggshells.

Mr. Gavanski, who was a vegetarian, would arrive on the scene in a burst of noise, gasping, steaming like a hot frankfurter, chilled by the snowy winter night that he carried into our room in handfuls or pushed in front of him like a snowball. Once he had shaken off the surplus steam, closed all the valves, rubbed his hands, and removed his coat with its fur collar, he would begin to take fruit out of his pockets like a magician. While this ritual was going on, my father would be lining up the chessmen and waiting in ambush with his English opening. Mr. Gavanski's magic tricks and childish games did not interest him. For me and for my sister Anna, on the other hand, this was a sight worthy of respect and admiration. The very fact that Mr. Gavanski was a vegetarian, a person in collusion with the plant world, was enough to provoke all my curiosity. He would stand in the center of the room, bracing himself firmly on both legs as though some exceptional strain were required, waiting for the silence and astonishment to reach a climax. When my mother stopped breathing and Anna and I were gaping with curiosity, he would shove his hands into the pockets of his coat with theatrical, highly calculated gestures and proceed to dig out a wide variety of fruits, from the most ordinary—such as slices of dried apples and amber-tinted raisins—to the most bizarre —such as dates and kumquats. The effect was always extraordinary, not only because the season was winter, when fruit fragrances in themselves embody something magical and enchanting, but also because Mr. Gavanski was acting like a master of black magic in extracting from his pockets such a quantity of dried but still fragrant fruit, fruit that had hardly lost any of its character. Our table quickly turned into a rich banquet, the fragrances mixing in an intoxicating way and ennobling each other. We had to rub our eyes, as we would at a circus show, and we sometimes had the impression that Mr. Gavanski was going beyond the bounds of the permissible, trying—as though we were in some provincial night club —to deceive us with a collective hallucination. Once he had released us from these magical fetters of sight and hearing, we felt that we might find ourselves in a very delicate and unpleasant position. And he carried it all off brilliantly. First he would dredge up routine fruits, whole handfuls of raisins, as a kind of introduction to the second part of the program, which would begin just as we thought that no further surprise was coming, that no further surprise could be coming. Then the pockets and lining of his coat would yield up dates, figs, almonds, marzipan, and exotic fruits that we distinguished only by smell, their names remaining forever a secret.

At that point, my father would appear at the door to interrupt the game, which he regarded as childish and undignified.

"My friend," he would say, not without a touch of malice,

"your artistic proclivities will lead you to complete financial disaster."

Caught in the act, Mr. Gavanski would drop the last figs on the table and join my father in the other room, where a fierce argument would immediately ensue over who was going to play the white queen first.

M y father had been vainly offering his new timetable, on which he had worked for years, for publication. The manuscript lay in a drawer of his desk, retyped, covered with red-pencil marks, crammed with corrections in the margins, glued-on inserts, footnotes, memoranda, supplements, preambles, replete with strange symbols and miniature ideograms. The ideograms were the ones that my father had cut out of his 1933 timetable and had patiently glued onto his new manuscript, giving it a special charm. These drawings were of railway cars with class markings, hunter's horns in the form of a stylized crescent, a knife and fork symmetrically crossed like the emblems on a coat of arms, steamships from which a slender thread of smoke coiled upward, airplanes no bigger than insects and just as light and noisy, automobiles reduced to their perfect cubist form and showing wheels diminished to ideal dots. This magnificent manuscript had absorbed all cities, all land areas and all the seas, all the skies, all climates, all meridians. The most remote cities and islands were joined together in this manuscript in a mosaic, in an ideal line. Siberia, Kamchatka, Celebes, Ceylon, Mexico City, and New Orleans were represented with as much weight as Vienna, Paris, or Budapest. This was an apocryphal, sacral bible in which the miracle of genesis was repeated, yet in which all divine injustices and the impotence of man were rectified. In this pentateuch, distances between worlds—divided so cruelly by divine will and original sin—had been cut back to human scale once more. With the blind rage of a Prometheus and a demiurge, my father refused to acknowledge the distance between earth and heaven. In this anarchical and esoteric new testament, the seeds of a new brotherhood and a new religion had been sown, the theory of a universal revolution against God and all His restrictions. It was a marvelous—I should even say sick—mixture of Spinozist pantheism, Rousseauism, Bakuninism, Trotskyism, and an entirely modern unanimism, an unhealthy amalgam of anthropocentrism and anthropomorphism. In short, it was an ingenious pantheistic and pandemoniac theory based on scientific achievements, on the principles of modern civilization and the technology of the modern era, and on the natural achievements of the earth's crust and the oceans. Yet it endeavored to institute harmony between the new materialistic theories and the occult sciences of the Middle Ages. However paradoxical it may have seemed, therefore, this *summa* of a new religion and new *Weltanschauung* was strict in devoting equal attention to the economic base and spiritual superstructure. Marx's *Kapital* was one of the foundation stones of this new cosmogony and social contract. Even so, in composing his imaginary timetable, my father paid insufficient attention to class conflicts and sociohistorical events in the world, paid no attention to historical time and space. He wrote it the way the books of the prophets had been written: obsessed by his vision and on the fringes of real life.

At the time when I used to unlock my father's desk to take a peek at the pictures and ideograms in his manuscript, we were all convinced that a new (the third), revised and enlarged edition of his *Bus, Ship, Rail, and Air Travel Guide* (published by Engl and Company of Novi Sad and printed in Djordje Ivković's shop) was in the making. A great deal of time had to pass before we found out the real sense and essence of my father's manuscript. Indeed he conceived it as a timetable, but as he progressed he became intoxicated by names of countries and cities. A wild, hallucinatory idea took shape in his consciousness, despite his utilitarian and practical intention of joining seas and continents. Clearly, for a job of such messianic scope it was not enough to draw a line between two distant cities and mark the times of departure and arrival for each train or ship. A mass of insoluble questions suddenly loomed in front of my father, a multitude of problems that he did not wish simply to ignore as had his predecessors in this field, and indeed as he himself had done in his *Urfaust*, the first edition of his *Guide*, the one dating from 1932, in which the international routes had not yet been included. The difficulties were enormous, and solving them was a lifetime project. My father had at first merely wished to produce a third, revised and enlarged edition of his timetable, a task that seemed simple enough to him. To assure himself of sufficient money and time, he gave up his job and began putting together a bibliography. Even then his practical sense did not desert him. He managed to collect a certain amount of cash in advance from his former clients, mostly Jewish tradespeople who had advertised their goods with so much success in his earlier guides. Of course, he was aided in this effort by the brilliant wording of the advertisements that, on the basis of exceedingly meager data from the telephone directory, he would compose painstakingly at night, by the light of the moon, like ingenious lyrical miniatures. *Thirty-one bells weighing 7,560 kilograms have been cast by Engineer Poznjakov's Bell Foundry. Make an offer, gentlemen!* One haikai from his collection, intended to advertise artesian wells, read: *With this pump, no more water troubles, no more bottomless wells. Adolf Krohn and Sons.* Yet another: *Ladislaus Sevar's renowned nursery delivers different kinds of roses, in autumn and spring. Erstklassig!* After getting the advertisements notarized through the copyright agency in Budapest, he would mail them to the owners of the companies, along with a notarized statement concerning copyright. Naturally, success was not long in coming. Once he had secured sufficient capital to allow his research to begin, my father supplied himself with new maps and books. Late one evening, in a flight of inspiration and illumination, he put down on paper the first sentence, intended as a preface or instruction for use. This glorious thought, this ingenious question came to him like the voice out of the burning bush to Moses, without warning. This one sentence, this great and crucial question, once transposed to a higher, metaphysical plane, would take flight with its sense and enigma, which my father had resolved to answer: *"How can one travel to Nicaragua?"*

Conscious as I am of the fact that I am demystifying the significance and magnitude of my father's undertaking, I nevertheless repeat here that there was nothing extraordinary or grandiose in his intentions at first. In the beginning, as I said, these were modest tourist baedekers containing notations on landmarks, museums, fountains, and monuments, sometimes including brief commentaries on customs, religion, history, the arts, and culture. But once my father had started consulting encyclopedias and lexicons for this purpose (he got most out of the fifteen-volume *Meyerlexikon* of 1867 and the new edition of 1924–30, plus the *Encyclopaedia Britannica* and the five-volume *Judische Lexikon* of 1928), the questions to which he sought answers began to carry him afield both in depth and in breadth, and he assembled an enormous listing of literature in the most diverse disciplines, in almost all European languages, and the lexicons came to be replaced by alchemical studies, anthropological studies, anthroposophical studies, archeological studies, studies in the doctrine of art for art's sake, astrological studies, astronomical studies, studies

37

in autobiography, cabalistic studies, Cartesian studies, cartographic, cataleptic, cataplectic, causalistic, causistic, characterological studies, studies in chiromancy, comedic studies, comparativistic, Confucian, constitutionalistic, cosmic, cosmogonic, cosmographic, cosmological, cynological, Darwinistic, deistic, dialectical studies, studies in dichotomy, diathetic studies, diluvial, diplomatic, dualistic, dynamic, eclectic, ecliptic, ecological, economic, embolismic, embryological, emotionalistic, empirical studies, studies in empirical criticism, studies in empirical monism, empiricist studies, encyclopedic, endemic, entomological, Epicurean, epizootic, equilibristic, erotic, eschatological, esoteric, Esperantist, essentialist, esthetic, ethical, ethnic, ethnographic, ethnological, etiological, etymological, euphonic, eugenic, evangelistic, evolutionist, exact, exorcistic, ecosmotic, fatalistic, fetishistic, financial studies, studies of florilegia, folkloric studies, formalistic, Freudian, genealogical, genetic, geocentric, geodetic studies, studies in geognosy, geographic studies, geological, geometrical, geophysical, geopolitical, geothermic, geotropic, Germanic studies, studies in glaciology, studies in gnosiology, gnostic studies, grammatical, harmonic, Hegelian, heliocentric, Hellenistic, hemotherapeutic, Herculean, heterosexual studies, studies in Hinduism, historical studies, humanistic, hydraulic studies, studies in hydraulic engineering, hydrodynamic studies, hydrographic, hypnotic, hypological, iconoclastic, iconographic studies, studies in iconolatry, idealistic studies, ideographic, illusionist, indeterministic, individualistic, intuitionist, irrationalistic studies, studies in Judeophobia, juridical studies, Lamarckian, lexicographical, lexicological, literary, Machist, magical, magnetic, martyrological, Marxist, Masonic, materialistic studies, studies in mechanical therapy, medieval studies, Mephistophelian, mercantilist, metamorphic studies, studies in metempsychosis, microbiological studies, mineralogical, monotheistic, moral, morphological, musicological, mystical, mythological, navigational, neo-Kantian, normative, numismatic, objectivistic, onomastic, optical, oratorical studies, studies in organography, orometric studies, osmological, paleographic, paleontological, paleophytological, pantheistic, parasitological, particularistic studies, studies of pedigrees, phantasmagoric studies, phantasmic, pharisaical, phenological, phenomenological, philological, philosophical, phylogenetic, physical, physiognomical, pietistic, Platonist, pluralistic, political, polymorphic, quietist, scholastic studies, studies in Socratic dialogue, semasiological studies, sensualistic studies, studies in skepticism, sociological studies, solipsistic, sophistic, spiritualistic studies, studies in Stoicism, supranaturalistic studies, Taoist, tautological, technical, tectonic, telepathic, theological, thermodynamic, topographical, toponymic, toxicological studies, studies in unanimism, uranographic studies, studies in urbanism, urological studies, utopistic, venereological studies, studies in versification, voluntaristic studies, vulcanological, Zionist, zoogeographical, zoographic, zoological studies. Notes at the bottom of pages and all the ideograms—crosses, crescents, asterisks—were supplanted by whole pages of manuscript in a tight hand. Abbreviations became subchapters, subchapters became chapters. The original idea of a combined guidebook-baedeker had become just a tiny, provocatory reproductive cell that was dividing, like a primitive organism, in geometrical progression. In the end, all that remained of the *Bus, Ship, Rail, and Air Travel Guide* was a shriveled cocoon, an ideogram, a bracket, an abbreviation here and there. In the meantime, the underlying text and marginalia and footnotes had absorbed this delicate, utilitarian, unstable structure that now stood almost invisible and wholly adjunct on the varicolored map of the world of essence, and this fabricated and abstract prototopic was represented only by the thin lines of meridians and parallels in the immense structure of some eight hundred pages, single-spaced.

The text stubbornly, obstinately retained its original title as a travel guide, reflecting the sick confusion in my father's mind: he actually believed that some publishers would be fooled by this obvious fraud and publish his chaotic compendium under the guise of an innocent timetable-travelogue.

Although my father regarded his masterpiece as incomplete, he submitted it to the publisher because my mother gave him to understand that we were heading into autumn and winter completely unprepared. Because my father had long since missed the deadline specified by his contract, and turned in an unfinished manuscript besides, the publisher rejected it. Moreover, my father had to return his advance and pay legal fees. Having lost all the lawsuits, he fell into a deep depression, which in the absence of any other, more natural explanation, we regarded for some time as the consequence of his failure with the travel guide. Only much later did I understand that my father would fall into a depression in the autumn and not emerge from it until the spring. During those transitional intervals, he would sink into profound meditation and would break off all contact with the world, giving himself over completely to his work. In the beginning, he would lock himself up in his room, to which we were all denied access. Later, he would go off on long trips, the meaning and purpose of which I was never able to figure out. He would leave secretly, late at night, without saying good-by. Our mother would tell us in the morning, in a voice that always sounded secretive to me, that our father had "left for a long period, in an unknown direction." In the spring, he would come back, thinner, somehow strangely taller, and changed. He would grin at us from a distance, waving out the window of the fiacre. It's all over, you would think. For a few days, he would be tranquil, enigmatically silent, then, suddenly, without any real reason, he would start roaring like a wild beast and shake his cane among the glassware. In the spring, he would recover from his lethargy, stir from his contemplation, shun his damn manuscript for a while and arrive at his natural state of irritability and rebellion against the world and against natural phenomena, which in essence was his true self. Terribly thwarted in the autumn and winter, deadened in summer, in the spring his egoism would awaken his once inadequately defined revolt against world order and people, and this rebelliousness, this surplus energy, this restlessness of mind and blood would bring him back to life. His was an unhealthy ecstasy, an intoxication of sun and alcohol, an awareness of universal growth that served only to irritate him even more intensely. Yet my father's egoism was really only a part of his *Weltanschauung*, his pantheism. His egoism had no bounds. In his panegoism, everything was subordinated, everything was meant to be subordinated to him, as in the characters of the Old Testament usurpers. And so, while the powers and energies of springtime were bringing nature to bloom, my father felt still more intensely the weight of the injustice inflicted on him by God and man alike. His metaphysical revolt, this belated monstrous offshoot of his lost youth, blossomed in spring with greater force, rose up volcanically, like an abscess.

Conscious of the danger of my father's messianic timetable, which had been placed on the Index by the new order (for its liberal and revolutionary ideas), we had to leave the street lined with wild chestnut trees. We moved into a small bungalow in the most miserable part of town, in an area where housing had been built without permits, full of gypsies, hoboes, and lumpenproletariat, as my father used to call them. There was a railroad embankment some ten feet from the house, over which trains roared by every few minutes, shaking the house to its foundations. This kept us in a state of constant tension, and we would cover our ears and hide under the covers, on the verge of a nervous breakdown. The roar of the trains would cut us off in mid-sentence and turn our most innocent conversations into violent quarrels, and we would raise our voices to a roar, incapable of understanding one another, waving our arms in front of one another's eyes, the veins of our necks dangerously swollen. It was some time before we finally discovered certain acoustic laws that saved us from complete madness and enabled us to return to relative tranquillity: when a train passed by, we would lower our voices a decibel or two and speak with an intonation entirely different from that forced on us by the sound of the train. We would talk from our stomachs, as it were, bending our heads and doubling our chins.

At first my father's job was clearing ruins. He had filed a sharp protest, however, justifying his disability over some ten pages of closely spaced handwriting, buttressed by statements from witnesses and discharge papers from clinics for nervous diseases. His arguments were irrefutable, particularly if we take into consideration—aside from the actual facts—his polemical tone and his brilliant style. "I hereby state for the attention of the esteemed Commissarist," he wrote in his appeal, "in connection with Item A-2, in which I took the liberty of citing the causes of my total incapacity and proving—if in a very sensible fashion—my abnormality as well as my complete mental and physical worthlessness, the worthlessness of a neurotic and alcoholic incapable of taking care of his family or himself, I hereby state, therefore, with a view to the most specific information possible on this matter, although each and every one of the aforementioned matters is in itself a physical amputation, I am stating that I am also flat-footed, a certificate to which effect I am appending from the draft board at Zalaegerszeg, by which I am exempt from military service by virtue of 100 percent flat-footedness. . . ."

More than twenty days passed, no answer came. The reasons were clear. Instead of publicly renouncing his prohibited book, if only formally, my father had designated alcohol and madness as the causes of his disability, plus the comical pretext of his flat-footedness. He would come home in the evening, frightfully exhausted, with bloody calluses on his hands, and fall into bed without a word. He did not even have the strength, as he had recently, to break the china with his cane. He was completely unarmed. He was forced to go to work without his cane, and he would return half-blind from the dust that collected on his glasses, which his rigid, cruel guards would not let him wipe off.

We became so accustomed to the passage of the trains that we began to gauge time by the timetable, that big alarm clock full of caprices. Each night, half-asleep, we would suddenly hear the crystalline pianissimo of the glassware in the china closets, then the house would begin to shake, and the train would cut up our room with those huge bright squares of its windows advancing with a frenzy. This further augmented our yearning for distance, our illusion of flight. During that year by the railroad embankment, at the time of my father's complete disaster, distance meant for us not only some faraway lyrical splendor but also the exceedingly utilitarian idea of running away, the deliverance from fear and hunger. Yet the thought of flight just exacerbated our vertigo: we began to live in our room as though it were a train. Naturally, the idea had originated with my father. We kept our belongings, packed in suitcases, we drank tea from the thermos. All day long, with my father gone, we dozed next to one another behind the closed curtains, wrapped up in blankets as though we were traveling.

Under the impact of these events, from which only some ethereal haze reached me, since my mother was herself helpless and disoriented, I fell into a kind of childish melancholy, lost my appetite, burned my butterfly album in a fit of hysteria, and lay on my bed all day long with my head covered. Severe and prolonged attacks of diarrhea had exhausted me completely, and for the longest time there was no way to stop it—although every morning, on my mother's orders, I swallowed a teaspoonful or two of ground coffee mixed with a little sugar. My mother simply could not guess the cause of my sickly lethargy and attacks of diarrhea. Only later did we realize that my diarrhea was the consequence of fear, which I had likewise inherited from my father. The attacks, which began without any other disturbance in my body, were clearly caused by my burdened soul, which was connected to my body in a sick way and which transmitted shock waves by way of the sympathetic nervous system and the digestive organs.

To look at the matter objectively, from today's perspective, hunger had a beneficial effect on all of us, at least in the beginning. My frequent headaches, which had been the consequence of my overloaded stomach, ceased altogether. My father underwent an equally miraculous metamorphosis: he became stronger, his gait turned slightly straighter. In place of the bloody calluses that had disfigured his beautiful hands, the hands of a dignified ladies' hairdresser, a dark crust formed on his palms. From time to time, he would slice it off with a razor blade. He was once again able to hold his pickax with his bare hands. Exhausted by the hard day's work, he would be calm in the evening, silent, avoiding outbursts of misanthropy. His surplus energy, commonly referred to as his madness, would be entirely consumed during the day, or perhaps merely exhausted, I don't know. My sister Anna somehow suddenly turned into an adolescent, ahead of time, no doubt. She was pale and slender, the dark circles under her eyes accentuated by hunger and testifying to the first signs of puberty. My mother, liberated from my father's terror and his support, reverted instantly to her normal agility, wrenched the curtains back from the windows, unpacked our suitcases, and declared one morning that we had finally arrived, that our traveling was at an end, that we were starting to live a normal life.

At dawn, we were awakened by a knocking that made its way into our dreams at great effort, as though through a wall. When I finally opened my eyes, which had been shut tight as if sealed by hot wax, I caught sight of my father in the gray, dirty light of daybreak. Barefoot and in striped pajamas, his hair tumbling over his forehead as if he were a concert pianist, he was bracing his cane against the door. The people outside were pounding frantically, and my father was sticking the iron tip of his cane into the lock as though it were an eye. We sat up in bed, frightened, leaning on trembling elbows, and looked at my father, who, the veins in his neck strained, his eyes wide with terror, was offering heroic resistance against the attackers. We heard men's voices from the other side of the door, voices still hoarse from the morning's freshness, low-pitched and ominous. There were women's voices, too, hysterical, sharp as birds' beaks.

As always in such circumstances, when my father had taken up a defensive and exceedingly philosophical stand in matters of life and death, my mother appeared in front of the crowd with a blanket wrapped around her, tall and slender, her hands raised. I heard her voice, almost unreal. She was saying something we couldn't make out, in some broken foreign tongue, obviously with none of my father's eloquence. But her appearance, her bewilderment, and her determination had an effect on the group, which began to split up, evidently moved by the strength of her argument.

By force of inertia, my father kept his cane braced against the door, resting his ear on the jamb and asking my mother for the password before he would let her back in.

Soon after, guided by my father's star, we moved to the suburbs, next to a railway siding. This was our third move in a year, and the place that we moved to destroyed our last remaining illusions about running away. The tracks were standard-gauge width and approached in a great arc from somewhere far away, and they terminated at the other end just as unexpectedly, somewhere next to the brickyard. The siding itself climbed all the way up to our hovel and ended there as in a gasp. The rails were bent upward at the ends, shored up by rotting poles. There weren't even any buffers. The track was overgrown with resonant weeds and dark nettles, interspersed with blades of fresh grass that was already discolored in spring, seemingly infested with the phylloxera of rust, which had spread this reddish epidemic in two vigorous veins, so the weeds and grass were sprouting up deformed, disfigured by hereditary blood diseases. Only some creepers found fruitful juices for their destructive feelers and for their poisonous serpentine glands. On top, where the rails must once have been as shiny as a mirror, they were covered with dusty pink deposits, like scabs. Rust had turned the iron into hollow, rotting tissue, into bone from which the marrow had been drained, split off in whole sheets from the sides, broken down into brick-colored dust, sunk into the earth, into the depths of the weeds. The ties had split crosswise, this reddish plague, like acid, having eaten them away.
This siding, as I said, destroyed our last remaining hopes.

It all happened like a miracle.
One morning, very early, my mother startled me from my sleep and told me in an excited whisper to get ready. The

few things we had left had already been packed. In front of the house, a train ("Wagon Lits Schlafwagen Restaurant") stood on the siding, bright in the light of its windows. Perplexed ladies wearing hats or slightly disheveled hairdos came into sight, munching white rolls wrapped in elegant paper napkins, which they used to wipe their long polished fingernails, and then threw out of the window into the weeds, where some sickly, unkempt chickens were rummaging about.

F days my father had been sitting stubbornly next to the coachman, suddenly strangely lucid, pathetically aware of his destiny as inscribed in his genealogy, in the books of the prophets. We changed sleighs at gloomy farms, hastily, warming ourselves with hot tea and cognac, and then fell into a deep sleep in the sleigh, hugging each other as the bells enveloped our sleep and our flight with a lyrical echo. My father tried to hurry the coachmen, offering them brandy, bribing them disgracefully, talking fast and gasping for breath as if he were being chased. He had assumed all responsibility for this trip, involving himself fully, although it was clear that he himself didn't understand the true purpose of our journey. But that didn't bother him. He only knew that he was supposed to *fulfill a chapter of the great prophecy*, for it had been written of him that he was to wander and flee "head over heels." So he grabbed the first sleigh and led the way toward the first settlement, circuitously, by the hardest route, indifferent to the fact that we were also being forced to fulfill his destiny, because the prophecies to which he adhered and in which he believed blindly were not exactly clear-cut, nor was he certain whether they applied to us as well. For our part, we submitted to his will without grumbling, assuming that we were supposed to bear some of his curses and endure part of his destiny. For days we traveled through a snowy wasteland, monotonous as the ocean, having lost all sense of direction. My father was steering our ship with a sure hand, hollering instructions to the frightened coachmen and staring up at the starry sky. From time to time, he would take a map of the sky from the inside pocket of his coat and spread it over his knees, just as he had once opened up his timetable on the train. Having ascertained our position from the stars, he would abruptly point a finger at the sky in the direction of a brilliant star, and the coachman—frightened by my father's madness—would whip the horses on. The coachman did not know that my father was searching for the star of his destiny, which was marked precisely in the Hungarian cabalistic-astrological study *A csillagfejtetés könyve*.

Finally we come to a halt, and my father pounds on the gates like a deposed Russian prince. I lack the strength or will to ask any questions—my eyelids are sealed by sleep and fatigue and I am trembling from some fear to which I have not yet become accustomed, the fear of unfamiliar places and unfamiliar people, the fear that one feels in front of closed gates. I hear the sound of the sleigh bells fade into the distance as the sleigh that has brought us here vanishes to the accompaniment of the barking of dogs. My father keeps banging at the gates, driven by some inner fire, some obstinate resolve. Keys clink on the other side, and my father pathetically pronounces his name, like the names of the prophets. The bolt moves. A voice: "There you are, friend, it can't be done any faster! We didn't expect you at this time of night." Some unknown persons materialize before us, sleepwalkers, roused from the deepest winter sleep. They take me by the hand and kiss me with parched lips, smelling of dark sediments. They guide us into dim rooms, light the wicks of the lamps, talk in voices still sleepy, low-pitched, rasping. A whole legion of kinfolk parades before me, strange, distant people with heads of dark curly hair, freckled, with noses like snail shells, and I kiss them one after the other, making no sense out of the whole scene. I feel particular disgust toward my paternal aunts, whose skin has a sickening taste, and from the slits in their collars, when they bend down their wrinkled necks to put out their cheeks, I catch a whiff of some tepid deathly odor, the odor of paraffin and of stagnant water from a vase of wilted roses. Only my red-haired, freckled girl cousins do I kiss with an incestuous intimacy, carried away by the abundance of their great heads of flaming hair and by the dissolute whiteness of their complexions.

With nervous haste, my father was endeavoring to fulfill his destiny, to fulfill the words of the prophecy and to accomplish his own redemption. The fact that he had made his appearance—as the Wandering Jew—in the place where he had spent his childhood, from which he had long since fled, guided by a grand vision, made him recognize the fate into which he had fallen, in a kind of *circulus viciosus* from which there was no way out: the arc of his life's adventure was closing like a trap. Impotent before God, obsessed with the idea that he was destined to expiate the sins of his whole family, the sins of all of mankind, he blamed all humanity for his curse and held his sisters and other relatives responsible for all his misfortunes. He considered himself a scapegoat. As a hypochondriac and a failure, he felt that his pride was wounded. He wanted everyone to understand that he was a Victim, that he was the one who was sacrificing himself, the one who was fated to be sacrificed, and he wanted everyone to appreciate that and approach him as the Victim. He elucidated his failure as a person with the fire from a sacrificial altar, on which he was consumed by flames, and he explained his suffering to his relatives and his sisters by his theory of renunciation. He described material riches in the name of his failure as a person, in the name of his sacrifice, and he proclaimed his own end to be the end of the world, the apocalypse. But it would be naïve to think that my father had been going about fulfilling his destiny without grumbling. Quite the contrary. He believed that no one close to him could or should survive his cataclysm; he held his destiny to be the destiny of his clan and his species. In a hoarse and gloomy voice, he foretold an apocalypse; with a single sweep of his prophetic arms, he enveloped the shops of his relatives, crammed with groceries, he pointed a flaming finger at silk, draperies, tapestries, and chandeliers; his eyes blazing with indignation, he cast an anathema upon dogs, cats, horses, poultry, and cattle.

"Who would have guessed that this wretch had entirely lost his mind?" I hear my aunt's voice, followed by the terrible, inhuman growl of my father. He had been demanding justice, stirring up accounts dating back thirty or forty years, citing figures and dates, names of witnesses and perjurers, in a voice that made glassware rattle in the china cabinets two rooms away and the dog in the courtyard howl frantically as if there were a flood or a fire. Every quarrel had to end in submission on the part of those with whom he had been arguing, or whom he had been insanely insulting; they would have to retract their arguments, concentrate all their efforts on calming my father, accept consciously and loudly and repentantly all the blame that he had thrust upon them, admit all accusations. They had to lower their voices to a whisper, because all attempts at outshouting my father were doomed to failure. He was capable of raising his divine voice to such a pitch and of straining it to such volume that all other voices were swallowed up by the turbid river of his baritone, and every attempt to outshout him merely provoked the opposite effect, for he would then raise his voice to an unparalleled intensity—seemingly without any effort. Before long his words, his divine howling, would merge with the tinkling of glassware and porcelain, the barking of dogs, the mooing of cows, and the cackling of poultry, neighbors came over in a panic, men carrying clubs, women calling for their children. When my father's voice began to reverberate like the trumpet of Jericho, everyone whispered in awe, believing for a moment that his madness was indeed divinely ordained. He, for his own part, would triumphantly resume yelling without descending from the pitch to which his baritone had climbed in grotesque rage and inspiration: ". . . with your greyhounds, with your carriages, with your shops . . ." An interpolation: "Eduard, watch what you're saying!" Again: ". . . in which incriminated heaps of nonsense and vanity have been accumulating, a crime wrapped in tubes, stuffed into sacks, piled into paper bags . . ." Another attempt at interpolation: ". . . our hospitality—" Again: ". . . and I spit on your hospitality, sirs, kinfolk! I spit on your morality! Pfui! After all, you welcomed me in the same fashion in 1918, and poor Morris, also a victim of your machinations, asked himself how you could be so blind to your own selfishness and your own worthlessness, how you could abandon your own blood and ignore the thundering of the apocalypse. And yet you dare to talk to me of hospitality. . . ." Another interpolation: ". . . if you don't like it . . ." Again: ". . . shall I leave? Of course I shall leave, and I won't be forced to watch your Lucullan feasts and bloody banquet tables, from which you toss us bones as if we were dogs, while hunger gnaws at our entrails! Listen to me, you heretics and sinners! I envision black days for you! Can you hear the trumpet of Jericho? Do you heeeeear? Or do you think those are Eduard Scham's hallucinations, his delirium tremens, his white rats!" Another interpolation: "For God's sake, Eduard, calm down, people are gathering around." But he was obstinate: "I don't care if people gather to listen, let them all come, every last one of them, let them come and see, let them witness bloody injustice, let them witness my just words and prophecies! For I say unto you, I shall vomit you out of my mouth. For you say, 'I am wealthy, I need nothing.' And you know not that you are unfortunate, and miserable, and poor, and blind, and naked! Woe! Woe unto you, great city, oh Babylon, impregnable city, your final judgment shall come in one hour. . . ." With these words, which rose in a delirious fortissimo of senselessness and exaggeration, my father lost the last thread of the dialogue; he called upon the Messiah for the last judgment in a frightful, prophetic monologue, in an inspired *lucida intervalla*, following which his voice began its descent into a moan, into a death rattle.

I am sitting in the sleigh, next to my mother, my eyes glistening, poisoned by my father's messianism. His words imprinted on my mind like a brand, I am beginning to feel the curse that is pursuing us, and I suddenly realize that the time when our days were intervals between trips, and our trips landscapes between dreams, is gone forever. I sit there, precociously subdued by suspicion, the twofold suspicion of knowledge. A short time earlier, while the coachman was hitching up the horses, I had followed him into the stable, where the horses' croups shone in the half darkness like satin. The odor of the stable, of withered grass and urine, reminded me of the smell of the camel's-hair blanket that we used to wrap around our legs in the days, so remote now, when we rode along the street lined with wild chestnut trees at dawn. Since childhood, I was afflicted with a sick hypersensitivity, and my imagination quickly turned everything into a memory, too quickly: sometimes one day was enough, or an interval of a few hours, or a routine change of place, for an everyday event with a lyrical value that I did not sense at the time, to become suddenly adorned with a radiant echo, the echo ordinarily reserved only for those memories which have been standing for many years in the powerful fixative of lyrical oblivion. In my case, as I said, this process of galvanic overlaying would proceed with a kind of sick intensity as things and persons took on a thin coating of gilt and a noble patina, and yesterday's outing, if some objective circumstance was suggestive of its finality, of the fact that it would not and could not be repeated, would become for me the very next day a cause for melancholic and still indeterminate contemplation. In my case, two days were enough for things to take on the preciousness of a memory. This was the same lyrical passion that we had inherited from our father, which was why my sister Anna would burst out crying after a holiday or a trip, without waiting—as it were—for those events to show how elusive they were: it was enough for a day to end, for an evening to approach, for the sun to set, for her to grasp that that particular day could not be repeated and to mourn it as a distant memory. Fortunately, when she grew older, by exceptional effort, she got rid of this sensibility and, through practical, feminine reasoning, reached the conclusion that since certain phenomena were inevitable she would no longer pay attention to them. I was never able to achieve that.

Our relatives, wrapped in colorful shawls, stand in front of the door, lined up in a hierarchy, according to years and dignity, their arms short, like clipped wings. They are waving at us with barely visible motions. They are scared by my father's anathemas, by the prophecies that had caused unrest in their souls.

My father orders the coachman not to light the lantern, and to follow his instructions. Then he pulls out the map of the sky from his pocket and spreads it carefully over his knees. With trembling hands he lights one wet match after another and mumbles, citing figures, astral or astronomical, giving us the shivers. Soon we float through the froth of the clouds, where the sleigh bells die away, where the sound of their clappers turns into a dull rattle. As we emerge from the clouds, through which we floated blindly, abandoned to the ingenious instinct of our horses, the sleigh bells resume their tolling and we catch sight of my father's star in the zodiac. The coachman is asleep, tying the thick thread of his astral sleep into double coachman's knots.

My father pays off the coachman. One mare shifts the weight of her body onto her rear legs as if to sit down, broadens her foothold, and urinates. The other mare follows suit, and we see a funnel being carved out in the snow and a liquid sploshing in it. The scene, not at all lyrical, has a degrading effect and destroys the pathos of my father's gesture and our meeting with our relatives. My aunt Nettie, an elderly woman whose head is shaking, holds a consecrated branch in her hands and offers it to my father as a token of her hospitality. My father's other relatives are lined up behind her, wrapped in thick dark shawls: Aunt Rebecca, with a great sheaf of black hair gathered on top of her head in a huge bun, as a counterweight to her nose, her long locks of thick black hair falling onto her temples, fluttering like thin coils; my uncle Otto, with one stiff leg, tall, slender, a degenerate offshoot of our family with thin straight hair, a shame for our thick-haired tribe; and finally, Aunt Rebecca's sons, my cousins, dandies who have brought back from Budapest, where they are being educated, the fruits and fashions of Western decadence—silver cigarette holders and high-heeled shoes. Their library, which takes up an entire wall in their room, is filled with horror stories and adventure novels, most of them published by Pesti Hírlap Könyvek. The shop, General Merchandise and Groceries, belongs to Uncle Otto. It is a dark, low-ceilinged room smelling of kerosene, soap, chicory, and camomile tea. Large enamel signs, blue and red, flash their slogans, short and to the point, on behalf of the chicory made by the Franck Company. On the other half of the door, a campaign is under way, full of dazzling promises, on behalf of Schmoll shoe polish. A serious-minded maxim à la La Rochefoucauld about healthy and radiant teeth, to which Kalodont toothpaste gives a porcelainlike sheen while filling the mouth with the freshness and taste of wild strawberries, competes with a piece of perforated brown paper, attached with a thumbtack, on which my aunt Nettie had written this Pythian and prophetic sentence: "As of the next Monday following Sunday of the week of February 11th, 1942, the price of sugar will be 200 pengo per kilogram, 230 pengo in cubes."

In the rear of the courtyard, next to the woodshed, is our new place, a servants' house, empty and dilapidated, dating back to the feudal times, to those remote mythical times when my late paternal grandfather owned a four-horse carriage and kept servants. It consists of two gloomy, low-ceilinged rooms with floors of pounded clay, which every spring thaws out, and takes on a false air of fertility, though it is actually barren, incapable of sprouting a weed. Resin mixed with soot oozes from the beams in the ceiling and hangs precariously in the air for a while, then burgeons and swells like a drop of clotted black blood. Behind the house, next to the tiny kitchen window that overlooks the garden, stands the whitewashed outhouse with its little heart-shaped opening. Inside the outhouse, on the right hangs a white linen sack with two roses embroidered on it in multicolored threads; thorns peer out of the roses' stems, like the cheap moral of some hackneyed tale. This miserable sack was the end of the line for dazzlingly successful movie stars, Viennese counts, vamps and heroes of scandalous affairs, famous huntsmen and researchers, heroes of the eastern front and glorious German aviators. Every morning I would find there, cut up in handy pieces, picture magazines that my aunt Rebecca had received from Budapest. I held in my hands the destinies of Europe's greatest wartime celebrities; people and events stood before me, stripped of their context, abandoned to the mercy of my imagination, so I would declare a scene from some German movie to be an authentic historical event, fixed in space and time. I would append mismatched captions to pictures—I would crown Katalin Karadi the queen of England, under whose real picture I would attach the cut-up page with the heading "The Ninety-nine Outfits of Katalin Karadi." I kept up with the world of fashion, I followed with the greatest interest the trials of spies, swindlers, military suppliers, I meted out sentences at will and granted mercy in regal fashion.

My prolonged sessions in the outhouse provoked suspicion and incredulity. My relatives regarded this habit as one of my self-indulgences, part of my father's legacy of introversion and slowness of the intestines. They recommended laxatives and sedatives, but at the same time they were astonished at my knowledge of Viennese fashions, new varieties of weaponry, royal scandals in Sweden, to say nothing of the incomprehensible bits of nonsense that I was able to prove with great vigor—without citing my sources, of course. Ah, that ingenious thirst for knowledge, that credulity, envy, clumsiness, ambitiousness! The scandals at the Swedish court had taken place for my sake, crimes and adulteries were committed to give me gossip with which to charm my friends: I was the demiurge of an envious, evil humanity.

JULIA is merciless, Julia invariably wins. She comes up with complete answers to the trickiest mathematical puzzlers —if a man walks five kilometers in an hour, how far will he . . . etc.—usually a thousandth of a second ahead of me. This tacit struggle has been going on between us from the very first day, violently, mercilessly. We both feel that we can no longer retreat, that we cannot surrender, that we dare not disappoint all those people who have bet on us so ardently, as at a horse race. She makes use of her charms, her feminine resources—no doubt about that. It is an open secret that all the boys in the class have placed at her disposal their money, their brains, and their strength. A whole army of ants is at work, finding answers that are slipped to her beneath the desks, bribing teachers, writing threatening letters, recruiting new followers, catching the most fabulous butterflies and insects for her, finding the rarest flowers and plants for her herbarium.

I enter the struggle entirely unprepared, relying on my ersatz knowledge of such things, all acquired from the picture magazines. I place all my trump cards on originality, lacking adequate strength or capacity for open struggle. Completely incapable of turning girls' heads with charm, force, or impudence, I decide on a fantastic step: to conquer Julia.

My every gesture, my every word becomes cagey. I lull
her vigilance. I count on the long-term consequences of my
cunning. To everyone's astonishment, I declare during arts
and crafts class that I am a total ignoramus in physical skills
and crafts. Julia suddenly lifts her green eyes from her embroidery, in fright, suspecting that some sort of dangerous
trap lies behind my words. Mrs. Rigo, our teacher, who
is up on everything, was herself confused for a moment by
this unexpected statement. "In the final analysis," she said
hesitantly, "everyone must conform to his or her own inclinations," thus letting me know that she had not yet lost hope
for my victory, giving me a go-ahead, so to speak. Relying
on recent developments in aerostatics and aerodynamics and
on the latest achievements in aircraft design (which I had
naturally gotten out of Aunt Rebecca's magazines), and counting on originality and shock effect, I built several airplanes,
very original ones, with stabilizers on the tail and wings, with
weaponry and all the rest. But I left the big surprise for
the end—although the design itself, by its boldness and originality, was sufficient to astonish. My airplane, thanks to a
little stabilizer skillfully camouflaged under the wing, was capable of landing on my shoulder. Anxious for me to succeed,
Mrs. Rigo gave me a wink, and I tossed the airplane up in the
air. I had carefully installed all the instruments in advance,
of course. The craft took off like a sea gull, heading toward
the light. And then, just as all the students were holding
their breath, it changed direction in an abrupt and unexpected spasm, made a spectacular loop, almost grazed the
window with its wing, made a turn around Julia's head like
an amorous pigeon, and returned obediently to my shoulder.
Before coming to a full stop after this dangerous and exciting
flight, it shook its tail like a magpie and then stiffened, devoid
of all its sublime traits, transformed by a magic wand into

a bird without a sky, a swan without a lake. I stole a glance at Julia: at that instant, she was ready to give in, to submit to me.

During recess, two more of my airplanes took flight, undergoing—in contact with gulf streams of air—the strangest metamorphoses. One, having used up its wings like a butterfly, dropped suddenly, headlong, next to a well. The other flew away high into the air, caught up by the north wind, and vanished behind roofs and trees. "It turned into a bird!" Julia shrieked in admiration, forgetting herself for a moment; then she bit her lip and put on an expression of complete yet false indifference. The boys ran off to look for the plane in the schoolyard in order to be able to refute Julia's gullibility, to turn her back from the dangerous path of exaggerated enthusiasm. They brought back a dead swallow that they had found in a moist lilac bush. It was almost weightless: the red ants had drawn out its entrails through its beak.

The boys lay the bird at Julia's feet, vassal-like, not daring to look up.

After my first victory, matters took a different turn. I conducted the struggle with even greater energy. Inch by inch, I conquer Julia's vanity, her mind, her body. At the beginning of the second semester we achieve a certain balance of power and I acquire more followers. Frightened by my sudden success, consumed by jealousy, the boys all take Julia's side—they trip me up, they denounce me. They accuse me of being a seducer, of not following the rules of the game. On the other hand, by virtue of the law of polarization, the girls begin rooting for me, unobtrusively, almost imperceptibly, holding off from revealing their preferences. Their assistance is confined to moral support: they encourage me with their glances. Incapable of open support, fettered by shyness and the legacy of a patriarchal heritage, they work in the background, sabotaging Julia's responses with sudden bursts of laughter, perfectly timed. The laughter spreads like an infectious *fou rire,* the girls stumbling around like drunkards, choking back hysterical tears, filling the classroom with bouquets of petards. Meanwhile, the boys remain cool, having understood the meaning of these acts of sabotage but incapable of acting on them. With tense impatience, they await Julia's decision, they scrutinize her face, which is pockmarked with concealed anger. Then, suddenly, a dimple forms on her freckled right cheek, her face contorts into a nervous twitch, she clears her throat, wipes her sweaty palms with a handkerchief. Laughter explodes out of her, painfully, like a sob or cough that has been held back too long, with a sputter that sprays droplets of saliva and with tears that blind her. Totally defeated, Julia totters toward the door, her body shuddering, her braids undoing themselves.

Mrs. Rigo is incapable of resisting this epidemic of insane laughter or of countering the infection threatening the left side of the classroom, the boys' side, where a symptomatic and traitorous throat-clearing is under way. She picks up the bell and loudly announces a long recess. The silvery tinkle reverberates through the laughter. The boys stumble toward the door.

Leaning against the wall, Julia is squeezing a tiny batiste handkerchief in her sweaty palm. Her crying reminds us of the seriousness of the situation, of the severity of the struggle. Selfishness conquers compassion in me. With a victor's pride, I pay no attention, I pretend not to notice anything.

No one knows why Julia is crying.

Who planted that sin inside me? Who instructed me in this dangerous, tempting preoccupation of a Don Juan? Who put in my mouth those seductive words, full of vertiginous ambiguity and alluring promises, that I whispered into Julia's ears casually, in the hallways, in the school yard during recess, or right smack in front of everyone, in the crowd by the door, wrapping my loathsome words in the sound of the school bell as in tin foil? I followed her with hazardous, menacing obstinacy, I spied on her, I enveloped her like a spider web, I slipped my glances down the front of her blouse as she picked up a pencil from the floor, I managed to catch sight of her naked knees under her dress as she climbed the stairs. I grew increasingly bold and applied the tactics of seduction that I had picked up from the picture magazines, I used the vocabulary of Don Juan that I had read in movie columns, I resorted to the jargon of white slavers and of night-club owners, I alluded to adultery at court, I spoke in the refined language of the pimps of Budapest, I took advantage of knowledge acquired from the horror novels in my uncle's library, I roused her curiosity and her femininity, which had been dangerously muted by the innocent courting in her art-for-art's-sake trifling with the boys. I succeeded in proving her complete ignorance in matters outside the narrow confines of school subjects and assigned readings, I was able to humiliate her, to make her helpless and ridiculous in her own eyes. In order to keep her in the power of my equivocal and tempting eloquence throughout the day, I made friends with her parents, who accepted me with naïve openheartedness, taken in by my skillfully feigned shyness and enormously impressed by my fine manners, my words and gestures.

One day that same winter, when I was sure that Julia was ready to submit to me, that she had lost her identity in the stifling hell of my fantasies, I resolved on a final step. I say "final step" because I don't dare admit that this, too, was only a part of my plan, preconceived and devoid of improvisation—that is to say, in the terminology of religion and the law, with premeditation. We were hiding in the hay in the stable belonging to Mr. Szabo, Julia's father. While Laszlo

Toth, Julia's page boy and court jester, was counting up to an honest two hundred, no cheating (Julia's words were sacred to him), I lay by her side in the hay, intoxicated by its smell, and I insolently declared—looking her in the eye—that she had no secrets from me: she was wearing pink panties. She didn't flare up, nor did she run away. Red blotches covered her face. She then turned her green eyes to me, which shone with devotion and admiration. She had granted me her little secret, and suddenly we stood very close to each other, having crossed the enormous expanse that had divided us until then.

With the shrewdness of a true woman, Julia ordered Toth to count again to two hundred, because she felt that he hadn't done a good job and may have been cheating. To provoke Julia's wrath meant for him to be worthy of her gracious attention, so much was he in her power, and he submitted with a kind of bitter enjoyment, sensing her unfaithfulness. Communicating with our eyes, we ran off in separate directions, fearful of the suspicion we might arouse. We found each other again in the hay, in the recess that still retained the warmth of our bodies. Julia pressed closely against me, free of the white gloves of her arrogance, freckled and green-eyed, her braids the color of rye. I told her that I was going to write her a letter.

"I know what's going to be in that letter," she said without blushing. . . .

Borne along by the force of aroused sensuality, amazed and frightened in the face of a new expanse of feeling and awareness, proud of the fact that we were revealing mysteries to one another, stunned to the point of dizziness by the anatomy of the human body and by the secret that was giving us goose pimples, we began to meet more and more often, to touch each other in a seemingly casual way, in the narrow crowded entrance to the classroom, or in the school-yard, or in Mr. Szabo's garden, in the haystack, in the stable, at dusk. Delivered into temptation in the face of this sinful giddiness, aware of the amazing differences in our physical make-up, in the smell of the folds of our bodies, delighted and frightened by what we had sensed but never clearly understood, we revealed all our secrets to each other, demonstrating them carefully, explaining them. We looked at one another as others look at pornographic books and medical encyclopedias, making naïve comparisons with animals and plants, like the first humans. Ah, those confidences! Those secrets! Covered with golden down like peaches, still free of the dark hairiness of maturity, we stood naked in front of one another in that paradise from which we were soon to be banished.

Our relations begin to arouse suspicion. Legions of agents hound our tracks, try to grab our letters, to catch our secret glances, to gather evidence, to seize us *in flagrante delicto,* to discredit us. Julia's parents receive anonymous messages that Julia and I are engaged, that we have pledged ourselves to each other, that we have exchanged rings, that we have pricked our forefingers with a pin and drunk each other's blood. Of course, these are the exaggerations of sick jealousy and envy, the products of fantasy and primitive gullibility, the fabrications and intrigues rehashed by village women on long winter evenings. Mrs. Rigo, fearful of the possible consequences, retreats into the cocoon of her formality and strictness, pretends to know nothing, to observe nothing. On the other hand, the two of us innocently believe that our glances go unnoticed, that our chance touches are our secret.

Our innocent adventure in love, blown up into a scandal, soon shifts away from the narrow realms of the earth and into the ether, races out toward the sky, becomes—I say this without any exaggeration—a heavenly affair, because our sinful touches, our inflamed pupils, the nakedness of our bodies and our thoughts, had been seen by a gray-haired old man with the horns of a faun, with a wrinkle in his brow, with a beard as white and curly as lamb's wool, a beard that we confused with the clouds. He would arrive accompanied by frightful lightning, the door would swing open by itself, and It—his forerunner—would enter the room, something quite indefinite, a voice without a body, eyes that flash out of the darkness, claws that stretch out toward my neck. I would scream in fear: "*Mea culpa, mea maxima culpa!*" He would respond with his bleating laughter, more piercing than thundering, and I would wake up drenched in sweat to hear my mother's voice: "You've been calling Him again, dear." My mother would then turn me over on my right side, thus unplugging my heart from the electric circuit of sleep. My nightmares would stop, for on that side I dream only beautiful dreams: I am riding Uncle Otto's bicycle, the nickel-plated spokes glisten in the sun, sing out like a lyre. Then I reach a ditch, an enormous paleolithic crack in the earth's crust, the bicycle springs up into the air, light as a bird, I fly without fear, full of ethereal joy, and finally I land in a valley, welcomed by a crowd as the victor in a grand bicycle race. Julia personally places the laurel wreath over my yellow jersey, which is imprinted with my club's coat of arms. I smell the laurel even in my sleep, its leaves stiff and firm, like coated bronze. Uncle Otto's bicycle is transformed in my dreams into a dazzling Leonardesque aircraft on which, borne aloft by confused prepubertal impulses, I have been satisfying my Icarian desires. By day, the bicycle rested on the terrace, coated with dust, and I sometimes received permission to clean it, to remove the deposits of dust or mud. I liked to see it looking shiny by day, the nickel plate gleaming: I was preparing it for my nocturnal journey, for flying in my sleep. I squeezed rags through the spokes as if cleaning between my fingers, I fogged up the nickel-plated surfaces with my breath like a mirror. Once cleaned and in its full splendor, spokes twinkling, the bicycle would sound like a harp. The very next day, however, in the hands of Uncle Otto, this ingenious aircraft would become dusty again, an exceedingly utilitarian contrivance which served to take him to Bakša, to Lendava, even as far as Zalaegerszeg, on matters of business and usury. His left knee had been stiff from birth, so he would fasten his right foot to the pedal with a strap, while his slightly shorter and deformed left leg dragged beside the bicycle. This lonely, uncommunicative man, who slowly dragged himself on his bicycle along the dusty rural roads, whistling, seriously debased in my eyes the glittering, divine aircraft, not only because he was deaf to its refined musical tones, but also because he turned the pedals with humiliating indolence and without fervor. Returning from his money-lending expeditions, he would load down the airy, crystalline airship with boxes of rice or lentils, he would even jam a whole sack of flour onto the rear wheel, causing the wheels to leave narrow, awkward figure eights in the dust.

In the spring of that same year, He appeared to me for the second time. This is how it happened. I was lying among some shrubs by the river, engulfed in sorrel, crawling along on all fours. The smell and color of the grass, the thick growth all around, aroused in me some of the pantheism and madness inherited from my father, and like my father, I wanted to feel everything in my power with my heart, with my eyes, with my lips, with my guts. Carried away by the richness and the greenery, the taste of sorrel on my tongue and a trace of spittle on the edges of my lips, I sensed suddenly that my thighs were beginning to sprout with unhealthy ecstasy—the very same feeling aroused in me by Julia's freckled skin, by the triangle on her neck between her braids, by the smell of her armpits.

He was standing on the edge of the clouds, raging ominously in the midst of an inhuman, superhuman equilibrium, with a flaming ring above his head. He appeared suddenly and disappeared just as quickly and unexpectedly, like a falling star. His silent warning threw me into the depths of despair, brought me to the verge of madness. I decide to resume the path of mercy, to become a saint.

The Reverend Father and Mrs. Rigo accept my decision with joy and reverence. The Reverend Father, however, in conversation with my mother, explains that my wish to become an altar boy cannot be met under the present difficult circumstances, the way things stand *today*. So far as religious instruction is concerned, of course, he is entirely agreeable, even flattered and enthusiastic, as he considers my interest exceptional, my knowledge in this area enviable. My mother bursts out crying. Mrs. Rigo stands to the side, proud and touched to the point of tears.

Stubbornly determined to endure in my resolve, I started to abuse my body, to whip myself. Whenever I had the opportunity, I would place my palm on the hot stove, or pinch myself until I began to cry. I pretended not to notice the picture magazines in the outhouse, I stopped reading detective novels, and, finally, I consented to read a book that my relatives had been shoving under my nose as the only real literature for boys of my age, Ferenc Molnar's *The Paul Street Boys*.

THE book of my life, the book that had such a profound and far-reaching effect on me, the book from which my nightmares and fantasies were recruited, the discovery that pushed my father's incriminated *Travel Guide* into the background, the book that was absorbed into my blood and my brain over the years along with the sinful picture magazines from Budapest, in between the likes of *The Captain of the Silver Bell, The Beauties in the Cage,* and *Man-Horse-Dog,* was the *Small School Bible,* published by the Society of Saint Stephen, "arranged for school-age children by Dr. Joannes Marczell, *vicarius generalis.*" They bought the book for me when I was in the third grade, along with the *Small Catechism,* from Anna's classmate Ilonka Vaci, who had written her name in it in indelible red ink. This Bible was the quintessence of all miracles, all myths and legends, great deeds and terrors, horses, armies and swords, trumpets, drums, howls. Tattered, with its covers gone, like peeled fruit, like bittersweet marzipan removed from its tin foil, the book began on page seven, *in medias res,* with the first sin: ". . . straightaway after the first sin, people found out that someone would crush the head of the serpent one day." Engravings in which the faces of angels, saints, and martyrs speak with pathos serve to point up the divine conciseness of the anecdote, this essence of essences stripped of eloquence, these events bared to the bone, this story line brought to white heat. This is an army of bad persons and good, the sinful and the innocent, people trapped in that instant of eternity which shapes or at least decides character, people marked with character like a trademark, like the brand of the divine farmstead to which they belong. Adam's face as he is about to bring the apple to his mouth: he is secreting mythic saliva, like a Pavlovian dog, as a conditional reflex provoked by the sour-sweet juice of the apple, his face puckered into a passionate grimace. Eve, our primal ancestress, is taking the stance of a village seductress offering the gingerbread cakes of her nakedness as she leans against the tree in the provocative pose of a fashion plate, sticking out her swelling hips. Her hair falls all the way to her ankles as if she were standing under a waterfall, her breasts are small and entirely out of proportion to her hips and thighs, she resembles the idealized female specimens in the illustrations of anatomy textbooks. A jet from that dark waterfall, a single lock from her abundant head of hair, has detoured abruptly from its course, twirling like a mustache, circling around her thighs like a creeper of some living organism, defying the laws of gravity, guided by an inspiration both divine and sinful concealing the nakedness of the primal ancestress, whose navel peers out from her fertile belly like an enormous, Cyclopean eye.

I stand bending over these engravings not as if I were watching a horror movie of history and myth but rather as a witness, as if I were in some sort of transcendental time machine, attending the events themselves. Bathed in sweat, aware of the far-reaching and painful consequences of Adam's action, I whisper, "NO! NO!" every time, because he still has time to release his grip and let the apple drop to the ground. I wink to him to turn around and see what I see: the python curled around the tree branch above Eve's head. But this eternal moment continues, finished yet repeated every time, and whenever I turn the page, I catch a new whiff of the sweet smells of paradise, paradise lost, the sweet smell of tropical fruit, I am illuminated by the balm of the sun and the azure of the bay (reminding me of our trip, when we stopped along the coast and I saw the sea for the first time). The landscape of paradise in the engraving, that brilliant work of divine inspiration, was not a picture or representation of events so far as I was concerned; it was for me a window onto eternity, a magic mirror. These engravings, these Biblical landscapes, were no more than frozen, isolated moments in man's history, fossils preserved through all the cataclysms, in the honey-yellow amber that coils around the wing of the dragonfly, along with smoke from the sacrificial altars, the sound of the trumpet of Jericho, the bellowing of the lions and the bleating of the sheep of paradise, the frantic hubbub of the Biblical mob, the roar of the raging sea, the odors of myrtle, figs, and lemons, the hoarse voices of the prophets.

I suffered in my childhood the destinies of all the Old Testament personages, the sins of the sinners and the righteousness of the righteous, I was by turns Cain and Abel, I was idling on Noah's ark and drowning in the sea with the sinful. *People had become more and more numerous and were full of iniquities. God then said to Noah: Build yourself an ark, for I am going to flood the entire earth. The Lord waited a hundred and twenty years for people to reform, but they did not reform. In the meantime, Noah was building himself an ark. Noah and his wife, and their sons and their wives, thereupon entered the ark. They took with them all manner of creatures, as God has commanded them. They also took along a considerable amount of food. Rain then poured down for forty days and forty nights, and a flood covered the earth. The water rose higher and higher. Higher than the mountains. People and animals perished. Only Noah, and those with him on the ark, survived. . . . When the water*

had completely receded, Noah disembarked from the ark,
built a sacrificial altar, and made a burnt offering to Him.
The burnt offering was pleasing to God. And He promised
that there would be no new floods. From that time forward,
the heavenly rainbow has become a sign of the covenant
between God and man.

I experienced this Biblical drama of the flood as my own
personal drama, conscious in moments of sincerity that I had
no place in the ark, so I would imagine myself trembling in
my mother's lap, wrapped in a wet blanket, or on the roof
of some house with that handful of survivors, aware that this
was our final refuge, and the rain kept pouring down, Bibli-
cally. I was consumed by the flame of repentance like the
rest of the people on the roof, as if on a coral reef in the
middle of the sea, while the swollen corpses of animals and
people floated all around us and the bodies of newborn in-
fants glimmered like fish next to the wrinkled, hairy bodies
of old men and women. And that man wrapped in a caftan
with the insane glow in his eyes, with his arms raised to
heaven, that must be my father, the sinful prophet, the false
apostle. And while the water inexorably rises, inch by inch,
turning everything into one grand liquid nothing, Noah's ark is
floating in the gloomy distance like an enormous fruit from
which people will sprout, and beasts, and trees; that great
laboratory of life is sailing away, full of human and animal
sperm, of specimens of all species classified and labeled with
Latin inscriptions as in a pharmacy, with a fresh crop of
onions and potatoes, with apples sorted in wooden crates as in
a fruit market, with oranges and lemons that conceal within
themselves a grain of light and eternity, with birds in cages
that will soon enrich the air with the tiny seedlings of their
chirping and will ennoble the wasted emptiness of the sky
with their skillful flights.

Once I accepted in my soul the day of reckoning, reconciled myself to my own death and my mother's, understood that everything is finished, that we are no longer suffering, that we are no more than swollen corpses in the sea, and ignoring for the moment the sorrowful consequences to which my soul will be exposed (I generously allot myself—at least in moments of supreme optimism—purgatory), I also experience the joy of surviving, the Columbian joy of the righteous man. Once the water recedes and the ark has touched the earth after so many days of senseless floating in the waves, I experience the most brilliant hours of my own fantasy and human history. The joy of living becomes so concentrated in me that I want to scream. I do my best to forget that this is not my joy, I abandon myself to this fantasy, this lie, I mix my shouting with the shouting of those getting off the ark, I gaze upon the triumphal flight of the birds streaking out of their cages, I listen to their singing, I listen to the roaring of the lions who are leaving claw marks in the still moist, cracked earth, I listen to the deafening thud of the hoofed creatures that are trampling soil sprouting freshly with grasses and flowers, new onions and sorrel, while the figs and oranges just brought onto land are bursting like berries, swollen with the weight of their juices and their role in life.

But there is an interlude in the ecstatic moment of my best fantasies, a divine entr'acte, halfway between the void and vital exuberance. This demiurgial instant, full of the most explosive fertility, as just before an erection—that is the point where the circles of nothingness intersect with the arc of life, that infinitesimal moment when one thing ends and another begins, the pregnant silence that rules the world before birds disperse it with their beaks and before creatures and beasts trample it with their hoofs, the postdiluvian silence not yet swallowed by grasses nor penetrated by the winds. This is the unique, pregnant silence, the climax of its history, the peak of its own fertility, from which the hubbub of the world is to be born.

On the next page the silence has already been shattered by horses' tails, trampled by the dusty sandals of Noah's sons, torn apart by the shrieking of birds and beasts, by the neighing of Biblical donkeys, by the wails of righteousness and criminality, by the birth pangs of the numerous Biblical mothers, of whom not one was barren, and their wombs opened up all the time like the school door, with clusters of Noah's powerful descendants issuing forth, chubby and clumsy fellows who just barely found time in their historical haste to bite off their umbilical cords, and they in turn multiplied like flies or rather like bacilli, by the simple division of primitive organisms, rushing to fulfill their great, messianic role. They grew like incarnations of divine concepts, like characters in some grand farce in which the protagonists have their foreordained roles to play, the proud pride, the modest modesty, while criminals and patricides were being born with knives under their belts. They lifted their Promethean gaze arrogantly to the sky, forgetful of the mercy bestowed upon them, and built high towers, defying the will of God: *Come on, let us build ourselves a tower that will touch the clouds with its roof and make our name a glorious one.* Then a swarm of angels flies in, swooping low over their heads, and with a single movement of their hands sow confusion in the languages below. Teams of master builders flap their arms hysterically, uttering gibberish, unheard-of words, fainting from fear and falling from the tower that is disintegrating in the midst of this universal, apocalyptic chaos of languages, of concepts, of words.

By the fifteenth page, the deluge is no more than a remote, mythical memory, the lesson of the Tower of Babel a utilitarian, urbanistic, architectural achievement: houses and towers are built without divine ambition, for human, worldly use, hugging the ground, occasionally as high as two stories. The descendants of Noah and Abraham are settling into them, numerous as ants, whole legions of bearded, sunburned males, hairy as sheep, talkative as magpies, lazy and dirty—packs of drunkards who have preserved only their masculinity from among all the divine attributes of the righteous, their Biblical bullish fertility, and forced to the level of a principle, to the level of a vice, they attack women and spill their fertile slime in abundance while the women, constantly pregnant, bring into the world future sinners in clusters, like roe.

Knowing myself, aware of my guilt, of my sinful thoughts and acts, knowing that curiosity is the fundamental trait of my character, curiosity that borders on sin, curiosity that indeed is sin itself, in my case at any rate, I experienced horrible crises at the gates of Sodom. In the false role of a righteous person, I assigned myself the role of Lot's wife, because her behavior seemed the most human, the most sinful, and therefore closest to mine. Consumed by curiosity, I was drawn to the magnificent, horrible sight of fire and disaster as houses collapsed and towers folded like dominoes amidst human wailing that rose to the sky. My curiosity, brought to an explosive point by the divine warning, was suddenly transformed into my sole trait, overwhelming reason and the feeling of fear, turning me into a weakling of a woman, unable to resist my inquisitiveness, and I would turn around abruptly with my whole body as if rotated by the centrifugal force of my curiosity, which had passed through me like a sword.

And when my brothers sold me in Egypt, I stood humbly among the strict, dark-complexioned slave traders, full of the quiet joy of the martyr, conscious that I was fulfilling my role of the righteous person and victim. The babble of the Egyp-

tian marketplaces, blacks, Arabs, Jews, mulattoes, the sound
and gurgling of strange tongues, the smell of exotic fruits,
the dust of the desert, the camel caravans, the sun-baked
faces of the Bedouins, the color of different climates, the
adventure of travel through the desert climates, the adventure
of travel through the desert sands in the company of slaves—
all this was merely the backdrop for my divine destiny, compensation for all my sufferings, the first act of my Biblical
drama.

By the twenty-seventh page, my role as Joseph is played
to full satisfaction. There is a splendid ending of trumpet fanfares, the desert sands have settled, the babble of the Egyptian marketplaces has faded away. Yet, a new role has been
assigned to me in this Biblical farce, a very passive role,
a secondary role if you will, perhaps even insignificant, the
role of Moses, and I experience what is surely the strangest
of my metamorphoses, a quasi-anthropomorphic flashback to
my earliest childhood. Of course, I once more become a victim, the most innocent victim in the world, victim of victims
(like my father): one of the male children of Israel thrown
into the waters of the Nile by command of the cruel and
almighty king. As always, however, I am the shining excep-
tion, the mortal who will evade death, the lost one who will
be found, the sacrificial victim who will come back to life.
My mother places me in a basket of reeds sealed with pitch,
she leaves me on the banks of the Nile, and in the insignificant but dignified role of the foundling, I become an orphan,
a divine *enfant trouvé*. When the Pharaoh's daughter, a dark
beauty accompanied by her ladies-in-waiting, hears me crying
on that blazing afternoon on the banks of the Nile, in the
shade of the swaying palm trees, I experience a sinful ecstasy
quite out of keeping with my role. I forget that I am a newborn infant. I forget that of all vital sensations, human and
divine, the most that I can feel and experience is the scenic

effect of the sun, which suddenly blinds me when the Pharaoh's daughter raises the lid on my cradle of reeds, in which I have been awaiting the fulfillment of my role, and playing a secondary role consisting of whimpering as piercingly as possible to attract the attention of the royal strollers. But that is altogether unimportant to me. Exceptionally sensitive to all scenes that include emperors and kings, royal heirs, princes and courtiers, and their female consorts, especially the female consorts, equally sensitive to the atmosphere of the exotic countries in which these royal tales take place, Spain, China, Egypt, I experience in an almost erotic way the dramatic moment when the Pharoah's beautiful daughter, moved to compassion by my whimpering, embraces me, when her slender companions begin intoning some lachrymose accompaniment on their lyres and lutes. I inherited this weakness for royal themes from my mother, in all of whose stories the protagonists were kings, princes, and princesses, while the rest of the characters had to settle for roles as stand-bys, a crowd of anonymous folk, from which only an occasional person—usually a beautiful gypsy woman or handsome gypsy man—would attain a more elevated role, on which the dramatic woof of her tales depended. My mother had been heavily influenced in youth by Chateaubriand's *Last Abencérage*, freely translated by King Nikola of Montenegro, and that influence remained undiminished throughout her life. For me, the happy ending to the whole drama of Moses is right there in that encounter, the drama evolves no further, remains frozen in the eternal moment of the blazing Egyptian afternoon, which to me is the climax of the drama. The future destiny of Moses no longer affects me. The continuation of the story simply lists unimportant scenic directions, printed in nonpareil type, apart from the framework of the dramatic action: the departure of the regal procession, the chanting of the princess's companions, the rhythmical swaying of their hips under the multicolored tunics, the sound of their stringed instruments.

The true end of everything is not depicted in an engraving. I say "the true end" because this is truly the irrevocable and horrible end, a sudden and unexpected cataclysm for all living things, although we are only on page thirty-three. But, as I said, this is indeed the true end: for me, for my book (I can read no further), for this Biblical chapter. Death arrives altogether unexpectedly, interrupts my reading, cuts the thread of my fantasy with the scissors of darkness, and that darkness, that gruesome darkness, is above and beyond the powers of the inspired engraver, who abdicates in the face of the grand, apocalyptic theme. The darkness is carried over into the ingenious picturesqueness of the text itself and the typeface, which are gradually drained of meaning, and then into the divine omnipotence of bare words, into the neurotic frenzy of italics, which now replace the curlicues and arabesques of the engraving. The blatant italic captions disrupt the cathedral-like restraint of the nonpareil like a shriek, leap out from the routine order of things, disintegrate in some sort of internal fever, burn up in the flames of rebellion and anarchism, are prone to exaggeration and excesses but are frustrated by the packed rows of loyal nonpareil, combining to become the divine Word, carried along by the senseless, Promethean idea of speaking out, of saying something about which there is nothing to say, which forced even the gifted engraver to abdicate: about the End.

But what I call the end is simply my eschatological conviction that my end is the end of everything. I am now allotting myself the final role, the role of the first-born (even though my sister Anna is older than I am), the first-born whom the divine angel-murderer is going to kill. The idea of perishing at the hand of an angel appeals to me enormously, of dying as humanity's martyr, as victim of victims, a tenfold death, because a tenfold death best suits my fantasies, bearing witness to my obstinacy, my strength, my steadfastness, satisfying my thirst for knowledge (truly useless) even in death. But let us turn, finally, to the Book, and let the Word be fulfilled: "Moses and Aaron appeared once more before the Pharaoh. But in vain did they turn a staff into a serpent so as to prove the divine origin of their mission, since the Pharaoh would not listen to them at all. Then God punished Egypt with ten terrible plagues: (1) The waters of the Nile turned into *blood;* (2) *frogs* swarmed over everything, including houses; (3) swarms of *mosquitoes* and (4) *poisonous flies* tormented people and animals; (5) a *pestilence* afflicted the cattle; (6) *ulcers and boils* broke out on men and beasts; (7) a *frightful rain* ruined crops; (8) *swarms of locusts* devastated the remainder of the harvest; (9) a profound *darkness* settled over Egypt for three whole days; (10) the divine *angel-murderer* flew through the sky at midnight and slaughtered all the first-born. *A terrible wailing and lamenting then ensued, for there was no house without a dead person.*"

We shall not retell all the sorrowful consequences of the divine comedy begun by a childish and seemingly insignificant intrigue. We shall settle for the most fundamental points.

Julia's parents gave me to understand one day that I was no longer welcome in the house. Their excuse was the loathsome suspicion that I had stolen Julia's water colors, which was their way of discrediting our liaison. "No one except you has been here the last few days, little gentleman," Mr. Szabo told me. "Those water colors were here, right here, nobody ever touched them." My oaths and my eloquent defense did not sway him. On the verge of hysterical weeping, I declared that I was going to take my case to God if necessary, that I would unmask the disgraceful schemers behind this plot and force them to confess. Righteous punishment will not pass them by.

But that was only the beginning of the misfortunes that came crashing down upon me. My sister received an anonymous letter describing the intimacy of my liaison with Julia with amazing exaggeration (in which I recognize, behind the altered handwriting, the sick fantasies of Laszlo Toth). This vile letter also contained a threat of murder by ambush unless I left Julia alone, which under normal circumstances would make me laugh, because Laszlo Toth is the incarnation of cowardice. Scared by the threat, Anna showed the letter to my mother, who fell into a deep despair, afraid for my life and touched by my sinfulness. Despite my desire to unburden my soul, of course, my confession does not go beyond this (which might be called an ordinary lie): Julia and I hid in Mr. Szabo's stable, in the same stall. That's all. Everything else is a product of a sick and jealous fantasy. Yes, I swear by her life, by my mother's life, that our relationship had not exceeded by an inch the boundary of the permissible and the honorable. . . . My mother, while suspicious, promised to say nothing about the scandal to my father, who had fallen into his quiet pre-spring depression.

The golden dust of time has slowly settled over this event. Julia's water colors saw the light of day, in the pockets of her apron, where they had been drowsing in the form of a dozen button samples, in the form of multicolored wax seals impressed on my indictment, which burst on their own in contact with the light and freed me of suspicion. . . .

On All Saints' Day, Julia received her first communion, and, cleansed of sin, as if emerging from a warm bath, she left the chapel dressed in white, a small mother-of-pearl prayer book in her hands, her braids gathered at the back of her neck, pink-cheeked from the shameful confession that she had just made to the Reverend Father. Did she recount to him the sequence of events, the craftiness of my schemes, and her own role as well? Had she mentioned the name of her seducer?

Exceptionally sensitive to the setting and *mise en scène* of church rituals, to the tinkling of the bells and the smell of incense, I was kneeling along with the other boys on the threshold of paradise, briefly equal with them, at least ostensibly, yet apart, marked by the brand that was burning into my forehead. I would not have been able to make that final step from pew to sacristy had it not been for the good graces of the Reverend Father, who had given permission for me to attend this solemn ritual of confirmation, during which our class—like a flock of black sheep—entered the divine steam bath and departed, bathed and bleached, leaving behind a pile of sins like a heap of contaminated pus. I sit there, overwhelmed by the frightful burden of my sins, I kneel on the chill concrete like a martyr, like a constipated sheep, the sin of envy that I feel toward my classmates coming out of the sacristy with faces lit up, a postlaxative glow and freshness on their cheeks, drips like vitriol onto my soul, constipated with sins. The solemnity of the moment prevents me from breaking into loud sobbing and from transferring my despair into a public confession before the entire congregation, before my classmates and their parents, so as to attract everybody's attention and pity and attribute to myself a full measure of importance; yet, at the same time, I don't venture to bare my incorrigible sinfulness, which is conspicuous enough as it is.

The solemn words of the liturgy, from the *Ad Deum* to the *Gloria Tibi*, trickle in their divine, incomprehensible Latin, interrupted by the dense silence of two-quarter pauses, like the white space between paragraphs. They continue to trickle, these sublime passages, paced by the rhythm of the little silver bell in the hands of the altar boy. A sacred dialogue—*Kyrie eleison, Christe eleison*—is under way, like divine rhymes put to human words. And I kneel in front of the nave of the church, stunned to dizziness by the smell of incense, which in this universal feast of the soul conjures up the calm of evergreen forests, the smell of pines and resin, and facing me, high above the nave, above the flickering, sputtering candles, a round stained-glass window is blazing away in a display of fireworks, like a hand of playing cards, kings, queens, and jacks. Mrs. Rigo sits at the reed organ with her head thrown back and eyes shut, strumming the keyboard, strangely youthful in a dark dress with white collar, the tips of her big eyelashes set off by a violet glow. She draws a whole scale of minor-key sighs, muffled and high, out of the black polished to a high gloss like the old-fashioned carriages, pressing the pedals as though riding a bicycle in her dreams along a straight wide road.

In our new surroundings my father's behavior underwent certain changes. I say certain because these changes were due more to the milieu, to the landscape, than to some radical transformation in his character. In any case, I had not previously been in a position to observe my father, and my curiosity in this respect had been completely frustrated by his repeated absences, by what I would call his conscious sabotage of my Oedipal curiosity. Who would dare assert that my father had not intentionally avoided any kind of personal disclosure, had not intentionally concealed his personality behind a mask, appearing alternately as a writer, chess player, apostle. To tell the truth, he played an unworthy role in front of me, he lacked the courage to show his true face. He was constantly switching masks, concealing himself behind the façade of one or another of his roles, all of them pathetic. Lost and hidden in the labyrinth of the city, among the multitude of felt hats and derbies, he was—thanks to his mimicry—entirely sheltered from my view.

When we moved to the village, my father could no longer hide. One day in spring, at the time of one of his sprees, I caught sight of him in his true form: he was walking along the embankment of the swollen river, returning unexpectedly after a six-day trip. We thought that he might have lost his way in the Count's forest or run away, guided by his star. As he walked along the embankment in his black frock coat, swinging his cane high in the air, swaying on his feet like a ship's mast, his celluloid collar yellowed, staring into space through his steel-rimmed glasses, my father became a part of the landscape, as if he had climbed into a picture frame, and he lost his air of mystery totally. To remain unnoticed—he must have seen me from afar—he hid his stiff-brimmed hat under his arm and attempted to slip by me. Truly a devastating sight. Without his hat, that crown of thorns, with his ash-gray hair parted in the middle, unsure on his feet, clumsy and flat-footed, he was entirely deprived of his greatness, he was nondescript. I didn't dare call him. The river had been swollen by the spring torrents, so I was afraid I might rouse him from his sleepwalking, genuine or feigned, and cause a fatal fall. Instead, I pulled aside and let him pass. He literally brushed me with the tails of his fluttering frock coat; I caught a whiff of the tobacco, alcohol, and urine, but his face was immobile. In this bare natural context, framed by fresh, uncut boards, his face came into full view, his magnificent nose streaked with red and blue veins like a blotting pad. Deprived of the baroque backdrop of city gates and the lighted vestibules of respectable small-town hotels, he now appeared in his natural state, all his power of mimicry lost. He, the chess champion, writer, world traveler, apostle, was unable to muster the effort to play the role of a peasant or woodcutter. Of course, it wasn't only pride, as he liked to believe, but also physical indisposition and infirmity; otherwise, who knows, he might have started wearing a peasant outfit and kept on hiding. Stripped by an official act of his standing as a retired senior railway inspector, with all its financial repercussions, he had come upon the perfect excuse for his orgies— he began to drink heavily, to spread anarchistic ideas in the villages, to sing the "Internationale." He soon became known throughout the county as a dangerous revolutionary anarchist, poet, and neurasthenic, yet he was also respected in certain circles for his wardrobe, his frock coat, his cane, his hat, or for his delirious soliloquies, for his awesome, penetrating voice. His standing was especially high among women café owners, whose very appearance inspired him and drew out of him the golden thread of his lyrical expansiveness and his sense of gallantry. Thanks to these muses, who stood blinking at him from behind the counter without understanding either his words or his songs, he was able to preserve his identity as well as his skin, because these plump, bucolic muses took up his cause with the police, opened secret doors for him, defended him from the village rowdies whose reputation as drinkers and singers he had seriously threatened. Standing on a table, like a statue of a great orator and demagogue, he would take a sip from somebody's glass, spit it out, and then—squinting as if trying to remember something—reel off the wine's vintage, its alcoholic content, the species of vine, its exposure to the sun, its district. The effect was always fantastic. Suspecting my father of collusion with his Calliopes and Euterpes, peasants brought their own bottles along in the hope of tripping him up and discrediting him. But he would spit out the wine faster than usual, with an expression of divine indignation, like a magician when someone peeks up his sleeve as he is stabbing his own heart with a sword. "Gentlemen," he would say, "not even the lowliest clerk would be taken in by your petty tricks. You plant counterfeit Tokay from Lendava on me, gentlemen, as you would forged money on some child. The presence of this lady"—my father bows to Madame Clara, who occupied the command post in the café, holding on to the handle of the beer pump as if it were the helm of a ship that lifts the foam of the waves—"the presence of this lady, as I said, forces me to refrain from spitting this wine into the face of your suspicions, from disrupting this marketplace atmosphere and the distrustful

mundaneness by which you debase everything that is sublime.
. . . I shall begin at the beginning so as to arouse your miserable suspicion to an even higher degree and make your ignorance still more conspicuous at the moment, at the grand and shameful moment when I tell you what the soul of this wine consists of, what gives it this false glow, this cheap ersatz taste, when I unfurl under your very noses the artificial rose of its blush, the cheapness of its color, the tawdry make-up on its lips, which I have just touched, gentlemen, and I am stunned by the degree of refinement with which they attempt to ape the true intoxicating spirit and virginal ardor of a Tokay. . . ."

This was the first act of the comedy that my father would act out in the evenings in village taverns, or rather a small sequence in his rich repertoire, into which he poured all the passion of his delirious inspiration, his whole genius, his ebullience, his enormous erudition. He would start singing only if provoked, and he would sing only to humiliate the village rowdies. He would burst into song suddenly, and with such force that the glasses on the counter would rattle and the village singers fall silent for fear of looking ridiculous in the eyes of the ladies. My father maintained an extensive repertoire of sentimental romances, old ballads and barcarolles, popular songs, and czardases, and numbers from operas and operettas, which he sometimes followed with dramatic recitatives, but in his interpretation the sentimentality of the words and melodies would take on a major-key purity, while the sugary sediment would be crystallizing in the silver goblet of his voice, becoming brittle and resonant. He added new subtleties to the tearful *fin-de-siècle* tremolo, purging it of its Biedermeieresque false delicacy and puritanical modesty, he sang without glissandi, with full lungs, manfully yet not without warmth. The effect was due primarily to the timbre of his voice, in which there were no petty lyrical affectations.

Instead, the notes rolled out in grand sweeps, slightly cracked like the sound of a French horn.

The third act of my father's long-run touring shows, which would last for days and weeks, like Elizabethan pageants, would end sorrowfully, like a tragic farce. My father would awake in a village ditch covered with bruises of unknown origin, caked with mud, his trousers wet and vomit-stained, without a penny or a cigarette in his pocket, an internal thirst in his intestines, and a suicidal impulse in his soul. Like Pierrot grown old, he rescues from the mud his miserable paraphernalia, his cane, his hat, his glasses, then desperately looks for a cigarette butt in his pockets, the last butt of his life, to help tally up the sad balance of all his days and nights, calculating the accounts from the bottom up. Unable to recall how or when he acquired the bruises, he sets about deciphering the figures marked in his own hand on an empty packet of Symphonia cigarettes. The dense column of figures, showing the results of all fundamental calculations, stands now in front of him like an Egyptian relic inscribed with hieroglyphics in his own hand—figures whose meaning has slipped his mind.

At last, my father is outside the frame of the drama and farce of which he is writer, director, and protagonist all at once; he is now outside all his roles, an ordinary mortal, the famous singer without his voice, without the pathos of his gestures, the genius forgotten in his sleep by his muses and goddesses, a clown without a mask, while his frock coat and his by now famous paraphernalia lie draped over a chair: the stiff celluloid collar, discolored like an old domino, the headwaiter's tie with a bohemian knot. The room is saturated with the sour stench of alcoholic vapors, feces, and tobacco. A large enamel ashtray marked "Symphonia" sits on the chair by the bed. A tarnished silver cigarette case. Matches. A bulky pocket watch with an old-fashioned dial and Roman numerals ticks off some mythic time, conveying its vibration to the plywood. Behind the frock coat draped over the chair, behind that black curtain concealing the infamous relics of a famous artist, a straight blue line of smoke rises and then swirls like a corkscrew. Although he looks as if he might have died a long time ago, his Symphonia is still smoldering on the ashtray, the column of ash gradually wasting away.

And where, I ask you, is his famous hat?

His hat, which sits on the table like a black vase, contains a kilogram of rotten beef—which he had bought six days earlier in Bakša and carried with him from café to café under his arm. Like carrion, the meat is covered with a swarm of flies and a bumblebee that makes a buzzing sound like the tolling of a bell far away, very far away.

As he lay there half-dead, his chin pointing upward, his jaws loose, his lips parted, guttural consonants, sticky and aspirated, wheezing out of his lowered Adam's apple, my father inspired pity. Deprived of the tokens of his dignity, the cane that served as his scepter and the derby that served as his crown, without his glasses and his fierce mask of severity and meditation, his face revealed the anatomy of his skin, the veins and blackheads on his prominent masculine nose, the relief map of his wrinkles, which I had thought all this time to be nothing more than a mask on the face of a sufferer and apostle. It was, however, a hard, rough crust, pockmarked and greasy as if smeared with make-up, dotted with thin purple veins. The rings under his eyes were puffed up, like blisters bubbling with lymph. His arm—his embalmed arm—hovered alongside the bed like the guardian of his body, a sleeping sentry, and was making an obscene gesture, the last bit of maliciousness that my father was able to concoct: making an obscene gesture right under the noses of the whole world and the dreams in which he no longer believed.

The following day, he had come to. Although still drowsy,

and tormented by a hellish, fiery thirst that he extinguished with water, he tried to restore his dignity by fixing his tie in front of the mirror, deftly, the way people insert false teeth. He would leave without a word, resuming his ingenious soliloquy, and return late at night without telling us where he had been. Peasants and shepherds told us later that they had seen him deep inside the Count's forest, some ten kilometers away from our village, or even farther away, in some other district. He would come home only to shave, change his collar, and catch a nap, speaking to no one and refusing to eat for fear we might poison him. He subsisted on wild mushrooms, sorrel, wild apples, and birds' eggs that he took from their nests with the hook of his cane. And in the summertime, we would come across him unexpectedly in the fields, his black derby emerging from the fiery wheat, his glasses flashing in the sun. He moved through the fields like a sleepwalker, lost in thought, waving his cane high in the air, following his star, which he would lose amid the sunflowers, only to find it again at the edge of the field—on his greasy black frock coat.

My father's lonely walks inevitably provoked the suspicion of the peasants and the authorities. In collusion with the local gendarmerie, and with the concurrence of ecclesiastical dignitaries and the prefect of the district, the people's civil guard and the rural fascist youth organizations took up the unpleasant task of shedding light on my father's secret mission, the purpose of his wandering and his poses. They began to dog his tracks, to eavesdrop on his soliloquies, and to file reports that were often greatly distorted and malicious, concocted out of somnambulistic fragments torn from my father's lips and, driven by the wind and currents of air, reaching the ears of the informers entirely devoid of context or verisimilitude. There was no denying it, my father's soliloquies were as brilliant as the books of the prophets, apocalyptic parables filled with pessimism, an unending song of songs, solid and eloquent, inspired, an inimitable jeremiad, the fruit of long years, of sleeplessness and of concentration, the heavy and overripe fruit of a luminous consciousness at the height of its powers. Those were the prayers and curses of a titan who had pitted himself against the gods, pantheistic psalms, based undoubtedly on the philosophy of Spinoza, the source of my father's ethics and esthetics. Yet one should not assume that his oral creativity, which derived from remote antiquity, from the Biblical eras of the Semitic tribes, was devoid of lyrical cadences, or that it was confined, as it might seem at first glance, to a dull Spinozist variant of Semitic philosophy. By no means. In this intimate contact with nature, amidst the lacework of the ferns and the prickles of the evergreens, in the smell of resin and the singing of blackbirds and yellowhammers, my father's philosophy underwent an extraordinary metamorphosis. Especially when compared with the principles and style of the so-called *Travel Guide* of 1939, which remains the fundamental, in fact, and regrettably, the sole source for the study of his pantheism. His philosophy began to lose its chill rationality, the line of argument was reduced progressively to a lyrical proof, which was no less powerful for being more acceptable, shrewder, stronger. The dead weight of heavy erudition fell away. The scholarly apparatus of antithesis/thesis, of thesis/proof became easy, practically imperceptible, enriched by the smell of resin, and the *quod erat demonstrandum* fell in the right place at the right time, like an acorn from a tree, while false and hard to prove postulates withered like diseased branches and fell off with a crash, a reminder of the necessity for reason and moderation. Essentially, my father was a modern version of the pantheistic hermits and the wandering philosophers, a Zoroastrian personality, yet conscious every instant of the demands of the time, fixed in space with absolute certainty, never for a moment losing track of which direction was north. Hence my father's devotion to his black frock coat and derby: the time of hermits in rags was irretrievably gone. That was also why he was so attached to his watch with the Roman numerals on the dial: it showed him the *exact time,* erasing the difference between the physical year and the calendar year and serving as proof and warning not to succumb to some supertemporal and nontemporal philosophizing that would ignore the urgent problems of the epoch.

Contrary to all expectations, it was the Church which displayed the greatest degree of suspicion toward my father. The authorities made shorthand records of their spies' reports and filed them in the thick folder kept in my father's name, but they did it with a certain derisive indifference, with total disinterest, sealing the whole confused and voluminous file just in case, with a physician's certificate concerning my father's unbalanced state, which freed them of any real responsibility in the matter. Still, the authorities were waiting for one of his outbursts to discredit him completely and to get rid of him simply and painlessly. The Church, on the other hand, possessed definitive proof of his disruptive and blasphemous activities. The fact that my father had second sight, that he was a clairvoyant and a madman, was evidence enough to the Church of his dealings with dark forces, because in the opinion of the clergy he was but a sinner, an evil force through a medium. The story went round, and was preached from the pulpit, that his iron-tipped cane possessed magical powers, that trees withered like grass whenever he walked in the Count's forest, that his spit produced poisonous mushrooms—*Ithyphallus impudicus*—that grew under the guise of edible, cultivated varieties. Before long the spying on my father was taken over by the so-called Women of the Third

Order, queer, devout village creatures who for their merits wore a rope with three big knots around their waists, bigoted widows who extinguished the fire raging between their inflamed thighs through prayer and fasting, ill-tempered, hysterical females who transformed their physical passion into religious ecstasy and superstition. In collusion with the village curate, they followed my father's tracks at a decent interval. My father failed to notice anything, of course, and kept on reciting his psalms with undiminished passion, staring at the ferns and birds' nests. My father's most devoted spy, Luisa, would sometimes mark down his words, sentences, fragments of sentences, awkwardly, licking her stub of a pencil until her lips were purple, as if she had been eating blackberries. With a fanatic's zeal, this "Woman of the Third Order" and war widow observed my father's every gesture, copied in her notebook the "mysterious signs" that my father inscribed in the air with his cane, marked the trees against which he had urinated, only to find those trees the next day "withered and blackened as if set on fire by heavenly lightning." Meanwhile, my father stuffs his mouth with sorrel, fixes his tie, sticks his cane into the soft earth, sets his stiff hat on the cane like a pagan building an idol, turns westward, raises his hands, and chants his hymn to the setting sun, the second-ranking divinity in the hierarchy of my father's religion (the first is the Sun-Son, the Sun-Elohim, the one that appears in the morning in the east, the prime divinity, Father and Son in one). Then he straightens up and starts to sing, to wail, clairvoyant and inspired, the pantheistic genius whose language and speech are becoming the divine word, songs of songs, and in the distance, shortly thereafter, the forest begins to crackle as flames flare up. . . .

The evidence against my father was rapidly accumulating. Under pressure from the Church, the authorities were finally compelled to act. In the absence of any corpus delicti, however, they decided to turn the matter over to the Village Christian Youth. They decided to wash their hands of the whole dirty business, not to enter the scene until after my father had already been crucified, to limit their action to a report, and if the need arose, to interrogate certain witnesses and arrest one of the participants in the lynching. They already had a volunteer for this purpose, a fellow named Toth, who was willing to sacrifice a week in pretrial detention, on condition that they put off arrest until ten days after the event, since he had to plow his fields in the meantime. The conspirators were familiar with his schedule, with his habits, with what one might call my father's personal, private life, except that such a term was in contradiction with his unselfish mission and altruistic intentions and actions. In any case, they knew for sure that my father had not renounced any of his habits, that he had gone out of his way not to lose the traits of a modern man, to avoid turning into a bohemian philosopher or village hermit. In certain details of dress, by eating three times a day at specific times, by taking afternoon naps, and the like, he tried to remain within the confines of the modern European way of life, he wanted to be faithful to the demands of the era, regardless of difficult wartime conditions and his own loneliness. And so they were able to surprise him in his sleep among the ferns as he indulged in one of his magnificent snores, which convinced them that he was sound asleep and that consequently his magical, demonic powers must also be at rest. He was lying on his back, arms spread wide as if crucified, his tie loose, ants traversing his forehead as flies drank in the sweet juices of wild almond and spurge from the corners of his mouth. Beside him, within arm's reach, his magical cane was stuck into the ground, barely visible above the high ferns, his black stiff-brimmed hat on top of his cane, slightly askew, like the helmet on the rifle of the Unknown Soldier or the scarecrow in a cornfield.

"Who is disrupting the sleep of the righteous?" said my father pathetically, sitting up.

He was perfectly calm, or so it seemed, even as he felt a double-barreled shotgun in the small of his back, imprinting a horizontal figure eight against his kidneys. Peasants armed with clubs, breathless and dirty, sprang up from the ferns. Luisa stood closest to him, her eyes blazing, crossing herself frantically, his cane under her feet like a poisonous snake. My father was still calm, his voice did not falter for an instant. He reached for his hat, then looked around for his cane. Suddenly he began to fidget, awkwardly shifting his weight from one foot to the other like a duck, his hands trembling like a drunkard's. To conceal the panic that took hold of him when he realized that he was disarmed, he fingered his hat patiently and then reached into his pocket for a Symphonia.

"Watch out, Toth," someone said, "maybe he's armed."

But my father had already removed his hand from his pocket, and everyone could see the scrap of newspaper into which he proceeded to blow his nose. Any kind of excitement provoked powerful disturbances in his metabolism and ample secretions of fluids. If he got out of that scramble alive, the first thing he would do would be to go behind a bush and urinate, breaking wind vigorously, I was sure of that. A woodpecker was drumming away over our heads: tap-tap-tap, tip tip-tip, tap-tap-tap, tiptiptiptip—it could be interpreted as a bad omen. My father had the same thought, for he turned his head in that direction cautiously, as if deciphering a message in Morse code. After going bankrupt, my father had worked as a railway clerk at Šid, so Morse code was no secret to him. Consequently, he was quite capable of receiving a coded message from a Morsian woodpecker and translating it in his head with substantial accuracy, not literally, but like a love letter written in an illegible hand. I think that was the only message he ever received in code, except for those at the Šid railway station a long time ago, before I was born. And the rumor that my father had a radio receiver-transmitter, by which he sent coded messages to the Allied airplanes flying over our village, was very likely nonsense. It was only my desire to see him in some heroic light, not just in the role of saint and martyr, that gave a minimum of encouragement to my imagination: he sits there, my father, flat-footed as a duck, the great actor, hero, martyr, he sits deep inside the Count's forest, tucked away in a cave, earphones attached, tapping the key, ti, ti-ti-ti-ti, ti ti titititi, suddenly omnipotent, holding the fate of mankind in his hands, guiding with his messages squadrons of Allied bombers capable of destroying whole villages and towns at one signal from him, leaving not a stone standing, turning everything into dust and ashes. Unfortunately, this was a result not so much of my faith in my father's heroic potential as of sheer fantasy. I had inherited my father's inclination toward unreality: I lived, like him, on the moon. But he was a fanatic into the bargain, he believed that his fantasies could be made into a reality, and he fought for it passionately. I, on the other hand, lay flat in Mr. Molnar's stable, where I tended cows, I lay flat there on the fragrant, fresh hay experiencing the Middle Ages with my senses. The rattling of armor, the fragrance of lilies and half-naked slave girls—the influence of literature. The flapping of green muslin on the head of the blond betrothed, my Julia, her hands weighed down with rings. The call of the trumpet. The creaking of the winch and the chains on the castle's drawbridge. I would hold my eyes shut for a second or two and then stand up in front of Mr. Molnar, my boss, pale, in green linen shorts: "Yes, Mr. Molnar, I understand. Chop up the turnips and tie up the calf." But what I was thinking was:

"No, Your Majesty, I do not assent to those terms. That is no good. We shall fight with swords!"

My father was beginning to lose his composure. He was not holding up well.

I could see that his body and soul were convulsed in a superhuman effort to restrain his diarrhea. He pressed his lips tight and glanced vaguely in the direction of the bushes, fearing the worst. Having recognized a representative of the district government, despite the false beard and salesman's case with which the man disguised himself in order to make an appearance at this dubious place, where a monstrous crime was about to occur, my father turned to him and him alone, surveying the rest with contempt and ignoring them, and began to explain to him the main features—admittedly in a very confused way—of his pantheistic principles, which had nothing at all to do with such worthless inventions as Morse's. "If these gentlemen had accused me," my father began, trembling and addressing the fellow posing as a traveling salesman, who had sought refuge behind the crowd, unmasked and ashamed, "if they had accused me of collaboration with the birds in the heavens, of ill-intentioned and tendentious meddling in the affairs of nature and its mysteries, even with the purest pantheistic intention of winning over nature and compelling nature into an alliance with mankind, not that mankind is worthy of nature's friendship, I would have understood their accusations. But the gentlemen are mistaken! What do I have to do with these senseless accusations, with these perjurers who ascribe to me certain human—alas, all too human—acts of malice? None whatever, gentlemen!" He now addressed himself to the mob. "I only preach in my temple, in the woods, my religion, which unfortunately has no followers yet but which will someday be revived. Its temple will be erected here. [He points his finger.] Right here, where you are preparing for a monstrous crime. Therefore, gentlemen, carry out your plan as soon as possible, set up a new and powerful religion, a religion above all others, enthrone by your act the first saint and martyr of the Religion of the Future. My tormented and helpless body is at your disposal, my spirit is ready in philosophical terms for crucifixion. Fulfill your intention, as I say, and the consequences will be far-reaching. Crowds of pilgrims from all over the world will come barefoot down the paths to that temple, which now glistens white in my mind and which will be erected over my burial mound. Tourism, gentlemen, will flourish like the weeds in the fields. Advance, then, if you have the evidence in your hands and a clear conscience in the face of Him who sees everything." A brief pause. "I can see that you are hesitating, that you are moved by my personal fate, the fate of a husband and the father of two young children [with his crazy eyes, he looks for me in the crowd]. Let us smooth over this misunderstanding, gentlemen, in a gentlemanly fashion. . . ." His eloquence and his demagogic passion did not fail him even in this delicate moment. At first the peasants had waved their clubs impatiently but timidly under his nose and interrupted his lecture with curses and oaths, but his eloquence confused them, and they soon began to listen to him, understanding nothing except that a genius was speaking to them, a madman, and mostly because of the enigmatic presence of the "traveling salesman," whom they themselves had recognized as the representative of the district government and who had finally removed his false beard, the peasants consented to my father's terms: if they found a radio transmitter in the bush designated by the Woman of the Third Order, they were to hang him on the first tree or crucify him like Jesus or one of the thieves. If they didn't find one, they were to let him go in the peace of the Lord and return his cane so that he could "follow his star." The official, flattered that my father had addressed the blossoms of his eloquence to him personally and had called specifically on him for a gentlemanly agreement, nodded his assent, and they all approached the bush. It was a magnificent blooming hawthorn that concealed an old fox den. First they struck the bush with a pole, and the blossoms began to stream down as in a blizzard. Next they dragged out a rusty old stovepipe, an elbow piece: rust had eaten away at the ribbing. *There,* I thought to myself, *that's how your father sends messages by Morse code.* Toth removed a cartridge from the barrel of his shotgun and put it in his trouser pocket. He banged his club against the stovepipe, at the neck, the way you strike a snake. The ribbing broke apart with a crackling sound, but without metallic resonance.

"I'm not lying," said the Woman of the Third Order, lifting up her skirt to show her rope with the three knots tied around her waist. "The Lord is my witness."

The woodpecker resumes its coded messages, and the peasants put their ropes under their coats. My father shifts his weight from one leg to the other, staring at the trampled ferns like a vulture. First, he bends down to grab his cane triumphantly, then he stands up suddenly, strong and tall, his physical equilibrium restored (his cane over his arm), he tightens the knot on his tie, taps with his cane the rusty poisonous mushrooms. Next, he takes a scrap of newspaper out of his pocket, blows his nose hard, and folds it carefully into four, then into eight, as if gold dust or aspirin were wrapped inside, holding his head high like a cock about to crow. You might think: he is going to put it in his vest pocket, next to his watch. However, suddenly he tosses it some distance away, off to the side. The paper flutters like a bird, and struggles briefly with the force of gravity before falling abruptly, like a stone, and vanishing into the flowering hawthorn bush. . . .

My father was in the habit of blowing his nose into scraps of newspaper. He would cut up the pages of the *Neues Tageblatt* into four parts and keep the sheets in the outside pocket of his frock coat. Then he would pause suddenly in the middle of a field or in the woods, rest his cane on his left arm, and blow his nose like a hunting horn. First a vigorous blow, then two weaker ones. You could hear him, especially in the woods, at sunset, a mile away. Then he would fold this scrap of rather heretical newspaper and toss it to his right, into the grass, among the flowers. Sometimes, when I tended Mr. Molnar's cows in the Count's forest, in places where I thought no human foot ever touched the ground, I would come upon a faded scrap of the *Neues Tageblatt* and I would think to myself in surprise: my father was wandering along here not long ago.

Two years after his departure, when it was clear to us that he would never return, I found one of these faded scraps of newspaper in a clearing in the Count's forest, amidst the grass and cornflowers, and I told my sister Anna: "Look, this is all that's left of our father."

QUITE unexpectedly and unpredictably, this account is becoming increasingly the story of my father, the story of the gifted Eduard Scham. His absence, his somnambulism, his messianism, all these concepts removed from any earthly—or, if you will, narrative—context, this subject is frail as dreams and notable above all for his primordial negative traits: his story becomes a densely woven, heavy fabric, a material of entirely unknown specific weight. In its wake the self-centered stories about my mother, my sister, and myself, the accounts of seasons and landscapes, fade into the background. All the stories stamped with earthly signs and framed within a specific historical context take on secondary significance, like historical facts bound up in a destiny that no longer concerns us: we shall record them without haste, when we can.

What bothers us and keeps us from giving ourselves over to the blissful recording of facts is the muddy tale of my father, woven together from one unreality after another. The term should not be misunderstood: my father's memory is more real than any other memory of my childhood, but he is artfully hiding behind one of his numerous masks, changing roles with unprecedented agility, concealing his true face, resorting to the most perfidious simulation. No matter. Let's attempt to unmask him, to demystify him, since—in any case—my father's story is slowly and inexorably approaching its climax.

To demonstrate to everyone that he had truly recovered, after that horrible day when he was almost crucified, my father began to attend to chores that you would never have expected him to do. He wrote letters to friends and relatives long since forgotten, he asked forgiveness from the sisters with whom he had quarreled bitterly a few years before, he put his herbariums and his notes in order. He even asked Aunt Rebecca, in a very submissive way, for permission to water the geraniums on her porch.

One day, just when we had grown accustomed to hunger and joyously reached the conclusion that we had "surmounted the crisis" (I naturally quote my father) and that we would now be capable of withstanding a prolonged interval without food, "using up the golden reserves of calories that the organism has been accumulating not just over the past few years but throughout life, aware of the possibility of—or, rather, ready for—such disagreeable surprises," my father came up with a truly lyrical outburst. Taking along his cane, the expression on his face declaring both a grand intention and determination, he headed for our relatives' garden and proceeded to cut nettles. He hacked away at the lilac bushes, and when he came upon a stalk of nettles, he would break it off above the roots, attacking the bush with his cane in his clumsy way.

"I never saw anyone pick so many nettles," I said in mock admiration, to provoke him.

My father looked up for an instant, and I thought he would respond with some maxim that would be instructive and useful in future life. But he didn't even glance at me, he simply loosened his tie and went on hacking away at the lilac bushes.

"You're doing that job very unprofessionally," I said, to provoke him. "You've cut as many lilac branches as nettles."

"Young fellow!" my father shouted, looking up again and then rising to his full height.

"You're doing that job unprofessionally," I repeated.

He was obviously confused by my behavior, which was entirely outside the bounds of protocol.

"You never had any understanding for your father," he said, furious. "You are beginning, in a manner wholly incomprehensible to me, to judge your father on the basis of certain external, altogether insignificant and atypical facts, on the basis of certain actions that are guided by the demands of a higher power, conditioned by reasons incomprehensible to you. Yet all of this is merely the influence of a low, provincial, rural milieu, which is very unhealthy for the shaping of your character. I understand, in the sense that I understand everything: you too, I regret to say, are teaming up with these provincials against your own father, you, my son, my Brutus, are teaming up with the sons of the esteemed Madame Rebecca, my ostensible cousin, you are under the influence of Mr. Otto and of the illustrious old lady—I think you know who I mean—and of all those who have resolved to discredit me in the eyes of my own children and in the eyes of the whole world. . . ." Before I had a chance to respond or defend myself, he turned around abruptly and began hacking away blindly at the lilac bushes. Then once more, altogether unexpectedly, he stood up straight and turned to me like someone who needed only to round out the conclusion to his irrefutable arguments, and I realized that this gesture went beyond the bounds of the forlorn role he was playing, that he was making a genuine and desperate effort to make me a witness to his martyrdom. "Andi," he said, "do you know how long your father has been smoking? Do you?"

"I do," I said, happy that at last he was talking with me. "You were smoking when we lived on Bemova Street."

"There, you see, young fellow, I was smoking eighty cigarettes a day. By doing so, I was sustaining my spirit and my miserable body, worn out by insomnia and hard work."

"You were smoking Symphonia cigarettes. Eighty a day. Maybe more."

"Eighty to one hundred and twenty a day, young fellow! Need I to say more? You are mature enough to draw some independent, far-reaching conclusions, to look upon your unfortunate father and judge him within the context of this one single fact, leaving aside a lot of other facts, that would illuminate my actions like a halo. Do you know, my young fellow, what it means for someone who has been smoking a hundred and twenty cigarettes a day to be left at a given moment—entirely unprepared, speaking in philosophical terms—without a single smoke?"

"That I understand," I said in a naïve tone. "But I don't understand what you are going to do with all those nettles."

"Fine," said my father, forgetting the nettles for a moment. "Although under the circumstances I am not particularly anxious to provide detailed explanations of my actions—these matters are much too tricky—I'll tell you what I am going to do with those nettles. But you must promise me a full measure of understanding. When someone who has been smoking eighty cigarettes a day . . ."

"A hundred and twenty a day, Father!"

". . . a hundred and twenty cigarettes a day, then, when such a person is left without a single smoke, without that glowing illusion, you must admit, young fellow, he is not able to inject into his responses and his actions the full measure of his intellectual powers and his lines of evidence. That much, my young fellow, ought to be clear to you."

"Good enough. After all, I'm a nervous person myself. I understand."

I felt genuinely sorry for him. It had been all downhill for him lately. He had abruptly given up drinking because credit was no longer available to him in the cafés. He could no longer charm even the lowest of the female café owners in the district. Nor could he go on smoking linden leaves mixed with spurge, with which he deceived himself in the beginning, stating and proving to his own ardent satisfaction that the mixture contained a significant proportion of toxic acids similar to nicotine. His celluloid collar was loose around his slender gooselike neck, and bright yellow along the edges.

"I won't ask you any more questions, Father," I said. "But will you let me stay around long enough to see what you're going to do with the nettles. From what I understand about smoking . . ."

"I'm going to make nettle soup," he said, straightening up so that I could hear his old, tormented bones crackling.

"As far as I know," I said, genuinely astonished, "nettles are fed to pigs."

I realized that I had gone too far. I could see that it took tremendous, superhuman effort for him not to howl. He swallowed, his Adam's apple like a bird's chest, bobbing up and down nervously. When he spoke, his voice was calm, yet full of tension:

"I must confess, with surprise and regret, yes, *with surprise and regret*, that you have completely absorbed certain lower-middle-class and peasant habits. You inject so-called rational, simplistic logic into everything, and that, my young fellow, signifies the most abominable ignorance in matters of a higher order. As proof, let me give you an irrefutable fact that is as clear as the sun: *nettles, my young fellow, were one of the delicacies at the court of Count Esterházy!* Do you still say, then, that nettles are *fed only to pigs?*"

"All the same," I said, "I bet that I'd break out in a nettle rash or something like that."

"Your crudeness and disrespect for the facts are profoundly

insulting and frightening to me," he went on. "I see in this a proof, one more proof, of the scope of the influence exercised on you by this peasant milieu, this sick environment devoid of any noble aims and concepts, this earthbound logic that sees nothing beyond the routine, this life and these customs lacking any daring or bold moves. *Yet nettles were eaten,* I repeat, and you will eventually be able to verify this point, *at the court of one of the most prestigious families of Europe.* Nettles were ideal nourishment for spiritual, artistic endeavors. Music was composed and played as nettle soup was eaten— *potage d'ortie,* it was called, and it ennobled the spirit and refined the ear."

Then he began pulling nettle leaves with his bare hand, making pained grimaces, and stuffing them into his black hat. Next he slipped his magical hat under his arm and marched home, like a Peripatetic devising a sharp response destined to become a foundation of philosophy and an adornment of oratory.

I knew that at least one of our relatives, with whom my father was again feuding, would be sitting on the porch, so I put my hands in my pockets and followed him, whistling casually.

Sure enough, if you had watched my father as he strode past our relatives' porch, waving his cane high in the air, completely absorbed by the weight of his thoughts, you would never have guessed that the hat under his arm contained nettles from which he intended to cook a potage of the kind that had been eaten at the court of one of the most prestigious families in Europe.

We were well aware that the nettle episode was but an introduction to a grand performance, an omen of catastrophe. My father had been harvesting nettles like a dog chewing grass before a storm. We kept waiting, as if in an ambush. Meanwhile, my father continued pouring ashes on his head and writing those long letters, letters to his sisters and friends, sometimes sagacious and didactic, sometimes as gloomy as a testament. But one day he put on his derby again and headed for Budapest, kissing all of us good-by, even those relatives with whom he had been feuding and who concealed none of their bewilderment and mistrust of this gesture. "We have to step up our alertness," Uncle Otto said as soon as my father had turned his back, "he'll bring a time bomb from Budapest." At which point an automobile pulled up in front of the house and my father settled himself comfortably inside and then asked me gently if I would see him off at the station. My mother signaled me to go along and followed me with a gaze full of meaning and warning.

I sat in the automobile next to my father and Mr. Janos, the hired driver. No one said a word the whole way. I wanted to leave the initiative to my father, to provoke him by my silence, to force him to declare himself, to tell the truth. He spoke up, however, only at the café at the railway station, where he was drinking a cup of chicory that he had ordered after a long, painful pause. I could see that he was having a hard time controlling his yearning for alcohol, which I took to be a sacrifice and a good sign.

"I am taking advantage of this moment of lucidity and mutual trust," my father began, "to say a few words to you. Appearances notwithstanding, I believe that you are the only one with any understanding of me, the only one capable of regarding my weaknesses (you see that I do acknowledge my weaknesses as well) from a profound standpoint and with understanding. . . . I know, I know, you cannot forgive me my egotism, my aloofness from the world. Perhaps you are right, but it's too late now for repentance and explanations. Do you understand? It's too late now, young fellow. . . . Let me say another word or two, though. My role as a victim, which I have been playing with greater or lesser success all my life

—we all act out our lives, our own destinies, after all—that role, as I said, is gradually coming to an end. You must remember this once and for all, young fellow, you can't play the role of a victim all your life without becoming one in the end. There is nothing I can do about it now. I'll have to do my best to complete that role with dignity right up to the very end. The forgiveness you will give me will be my redemption."

I must confess that I didn't really understand him. But I could tell that he was speaking in a slightly lower octave than usual, in an octave of sincerity that had long since withered inside him and that sounded unusual and moving. We sat in a provincial railway station café, the only customers, tête-à-tête, over a filthy checkered tablecloth. It was a late summer afternoon, and flies swooped back and forth, intoxicated by their own flight and the heat. The room smelled of goulash and floor wax. A celesta stood in the corner, covered with cloth like a casket. Flypaper swayed back and forth, gently and lazily, measuring out the minutes. The bottles on the shelves were taking their siesta, crammed with the sun's rays and their own weight, like flower buds or artillery shells.

"There are people," my father continued, "who are born to be unhappy and to make others unhappy, who are the victims of celestial intrigues incomprehensible to us, guinea pigs for the celestial machinery, rebels allotted the part of a rebel yet born—by the cruel logic of the celestial comedy—with their wings clipped. They are titans without the power of titans, dwarf-titans whose only greatness was given them in the form of a rigid dose of sensitivity that dissolves their trifling strength like alcohol. They follow their star, their sick sensibility, borne along by titanic plans and intentions, but then break like waves against the rocky banks of triviality. The height of the cruelty allotted them in lucidity, that awareness of their own limitations, that sick capacity for dissociation. I look at myself in the role forced on me by the heavens and by fate, conscious of my role at all times yet at the same time unable to resist it with the force of logic or will. . . . Fortunately, as I said, this role is coming to an end. . . ."

This unique moment of sincerity and lucidity was broken by the arrival of the train. My father left a lordly tip on the table and took his secret with him to the grave.

When he returned from Budapest after a couple of days, my father brought me a tool chest as he had promised that day at the railway station. There was a touching sincerity in this gesture. He swaggered around the house as if he were accustomed to giving gifts and performing acts of charity, yet we well knew what a sacrifice this was for him, how much of a proof, if you will, of the goodness of his heart, because it must have been an enormous effort for him to remember my wish—which I had mentioned more for the sake of decorum than in the hope that he would satisfy it. The tool chest, a miniature carpentry shop, was a part of my distant dream, the ornament of my inclinations, the wherewithal to match my inborn talent for carpentry, a talent that climaxed during my severest preadolescent religious crises: ever since I had seen the child Jesus with a chisel and hammer in an engraving in a chapter of my catechism titled "Concerning the Fourth Commandment of God," my passion had become more inflamed. The caption under the illustration, in blazing italics, read, "He was obedient to his parents." I associated this directly with carpentry, assuming that building wooden tripods was the height of devotion to one's parents and to God, symbolic, like a prayer or Lenten fasting.

Uncle Otto, still mistrustful of my father, took advantage of one of my father's afternoon strolls to take apart my tool chest, obviously with the intention of finding a detonator. Holding his breath, he cautiously unscrewed the handle of a drill, keeping it some distance from his eyes, trying to penetrate the secret world of all this paraphernalia, to peer inside, to uncover the diabolical interior within the harmless exterior. Large drops of sweat glistened on his forehead.

Uncle Otto was overdoing it, of course, in his sick fear for his life and property. Despite our doubts and suspicions, my father had genuinely improved. He was no longer acting. On the contrary: he had experienced his splendid *lucida intervalla,* a moment experienced only by great minds when calmly confronted with—philosophically prepared for, as it were—death.

My mother was packing my father's case silently, head bowed, the picture of piety. Clearly, she had forgiven him everything. Yet she refrained from saying anything, from doing anything to disrupt his marvelous calm, which merited respect. She packed the famous wardrobe of this divine clown who was retiring, taking with him his renowned paraphernalia. The striped pajamas, in which he had appeared several times in the role of father-defender of the home and father-protector (during the pogroms when he braced his iron-tipped cane against the door while frenetic pounding went on outside), and next to the striped pajamas, not unlike those worn in mental hospitals and sanatoriums, are his white shirts, starched and shabby, and next to them, like their ornament and their crown, a bunch of high celluloid collars tied together with a rubber band, shiny and stiff collars yellowed by nicotine; a hunch of black ties, elongated like water-lily stalks; a pair of imitation-silver cuff links, like a ruler's rings, with initials.

Who, I ask you, would dare to equate my father with a traveling salesman?

It was a wonderful summer day when he set out along the road. He walked down the great Roman highway, full of zest, waving his cane high up in the air, while we followed two paces behind, in deference to his tranquillity. But when it came to crossing over from the Roman highway onto a dusty country road, he suddenly began to lose his strength and falter, leaning his weight on his cane, an indication that his flat feet had turned disobedient and that his spirit had begun to wane. He would never have admitted that, of course, nor would he ever in his life have ventured to do what my mother now did: she stopped a cart full of gypsies and asked them to accommodate the gentleman, because the gentleman was flat-footed and would not be able to make it all the way to Bakša. For this favor she offered them her muslin kerchief. My father climbed into the cart, trying to seem reluctant, as if he were doing it to please us. But once he had found a place beside a young gypsy woman on the front seat (we trudged behind the cart), he suddenly became the old, magnificent Eduard Scham, straight of bearing, the picture of gallantry and contempt for wealth. Two mangy little mules are dragging the cart along the dusty country road, and inside the cart, under a torn tent, gypsy children are squealing like kittens, pots and troughs are clanging. A young mustachioed gypsy offers my father a puff on his pipe. Next to the young gypsy woman with swollen breasts, my father sits like the Prince of Wales, or a maître d'hôtel, like a conjurer or a circus manager, like a lion tamer or a spy, like an anthropologist or a headwaiter, like a smuggler or a Quaker missionary, like a ruler traveling incognito or a school inspector, like a country doctor or a traveling salesman for a west European razor-blade company. He sits erect, imperious, splendid in his Olympian calm beneath the dark crown of his derby, on which dust is settling like pollen.

In the meantime, at the home of the Rhinewines:

Mr. Rhinewine, a short, bald, stunted shopkeeper with a snail-shaped nose and short arms, head pulled down between his shoulders, stands on a chair, as if on stilts, surveying the scene with his narrow eyes. He feels overexposed to public view, so he bends over a bit, retreats into his hump as into a cocoon from which his hoarse voice breaks out. He holds a huge notebook for double-entry bookkeeping, holds it the way Moses held the tablets on Mount Sinai, and yells:

"*Eine Singermaschine!*"

"*Ja.*"

"One mirror, large, hinged into two parts."

Pause.

"One large, hinged, two-part mirror!"

A servant pipes up (in German): "Sir, we can't find it."

Momentary confusion. Workmen and servants dart in and out amidst the furniture in the courtyard and in the house. Mr. Rhinewine blinks patiently, searching from his perch for his mirror, which has gotten lost in this great migration of peoples, in this historical moment full of chaos, before the deluge. Mrs. Rhinewine, a stout, hairy lady wearing an old-fashioned wide-brimmed hat and dragging a train along the ground, wanders through the half-empty salons, totally at a loss, deprived of the backdrops in which she has spent her burgher lifetime, pathetically awkward in her senseless wandering, an absurd, anachronistic, parchment-white fan in her small, pudgy hand.

But everything is all right. The mirror has been dragged out of the darkness (it was covered with a Persian carpet), and the workers are placing it carefully on a cart, and in the mirror raised above this gigantic flea market there is a reflection of an idyllic summer landscape, of greenery and light and a fragment of bright blue sky, with clean white clouds floating, as in the paintings of the Flemish masters. The descendants of Noah, in their innocence, are going off to their deaths, as the Pharaohs went into the silence of their magnificent pyramids, carrying all their earthly goods with them. Carpets, tapestries, dressing tables, marble-topped tables,

110

precious antiquarian books in leather bindings, thronelike Biedermeier armchairs, couches, ottomans, dressers, dishes, glassware, crystal, flowerpots with rubber trees, flowerpots with oleanders, with geraniums, with Japanese orange trees, with lemon trees; silverware chests lined with red cloth, like those cases designed to hold dueling pistols; an upright piano, a violin case like a small child's sarcophagus, bundles of documents, family portraits in baroque frames lifted out of their dusty repose and deprived of their eternal verticality, thrust into humiliating, blasphemous postures, heads down or hopelessly curtailed so that facial expressions and force of character were lost; gold-pendulum wall clocks like altars, polished miniature alarm clocks like golden apples, large black umbrellas like furled funeral banners, multicolored old-fashioned polka-dot parasols with elongated gilt handles, swaying silk petticoats fringed with lace, scales and balances, a whole museum of the history of mercantilism from the Bronze Age to our times, zinc weights in boxes of their own and arranged by size, rolls of fabric, chintz and mohair-silk, gilt advertising cards hanging like decorations, each card noting price, item number, and the company trademark in the form of an innocent lamb or daisy blossom; mysterious trunks with heavy locks, elegant yellow suitcases and vanity cases smelling of tanned leather, swollen, stuffed full, their nickel-plated clasps shiny, held shut with straps; iron stoves leaking soot, along with their pipes—more to come. A billiard table, backdrop for a meadow scene, is difficult to maneuver through the door, no matter how much the workers shout and curse. It moves along inch by inch, like some accursed stone for the pyramid of Cheops. Next, a porter brings bowling balls, holding them cautiously in his palm like duck eggs just laid and still warm.

"*Ein Lüster!*"

"*Noch ein Lüster!*"

"Ein Halbzylinder!"

"Ein Frack!"

"Noch ein Frack!"

"Ein Frack. I said, '*Ein Frack!'* "

This enormous pile of junk, this onetime wealth suddenly deprived of meaning or context, passes from hand to hand. Dragged out of the dreary depths of dressers and dark corners of shops, salons, and warehouses, out of attics and cellars, these objects suddenly shed their value, fall apart in contact with the sun, darken like litmus paper, spoil, decompose, turn into a shade, into cobweb, into *reliquiae reliquiarum,* into dust and ashes.

Nonetheless, the cart fills up with incredible speed, the objects become part of the cart itself, part of its chassis, built into it as a kind of mezzanine. The cart grows, becomes multi-storied, rises high up like scaffolding built by the wisdom of ingenious master builders on the basis of *ad hoc* plans, based on some original inspiration. Add just one more straw and the whole ingenious structure—which is held together by the laws of equilibrium and the secret formulas of walking—would tumble down. Now the last item: a stainless-steel sink, freshly unscrewed, still dripping, is placed between the legs of an overturned chair—the final ounce of weight on the right-hand scale. The focus of equilibrium, like the invisible needle on a pharmacist's scale, is on a plane with the shaft of the cart, right in between the horses' ears. Absolute equilibrium.

Hop!

A gray cat has leaped onto the cart and made itself comfortable next to a violin case. It is all ears. The workers throw cords over the cart as if it were a coffin.

Now the workers pile heavy loads onto a second cart, sacks of flour and wheat, bags of corn, grain, potatoes, cartons of coffee, rice, spices, red pepper. The stableboys patiently shovel fresh droppings from under the bulky Styrian horses, who are stupefied by this human commotion.

They carry out the bottles and jars of preserves and jams, labeled by date and type of fruit; hams, link sausages, cheeses big as millstones; they roll along barrels of beer and wine and drag out cans of lard and cooking oil, huge tin cans flaunting the names of the great European monopolies, the dark, semi-Gothic letters resembling those on tombstones and signboards. The bottles clink inside the cases like cannon balls, the champagne is carried with caution, like nitroglycerin, the mineral water with which the porters are refreshing themselves is fizzing with a light spray, barely wetting Franz Josef's beard on the "Ferencz József keserüviz" label.

This wretched reworking of the antediluvian evacuation, this landlocked, earthbound reprise of the episode of Noah's ark, that Biblical divine comedy, is being played out consistently and to the very end. The descendants of Noah, enriched with experience, carry with them (in the fourth, fifth, and sixth carts) specimens of livestock and poultry: the hens cackle madly, the geese stick their heads through all the openings in the wire mesh as if knitting, wheezing in their simple-minded impotence and confusion; the canaries leap about, ramming suicidally against their cages, and the parrot, confused by the universal commotion, is unable to recall a single human word, not even a single curse, so he goes on screeching in his parrot language; the dogs growl and bark, proud as lions, and then crouch as if sensing a fire. The calves are calling out to their milk-rich mothers, imploring, pained, almost human. . . .

At which point Mr. Rhinewine catches sight of my father alighting from the gypsy cart.

"Hey, Scham!" Mr. Rhinewine shouts from his chair. "Where are your belongings, Scham?"

113

My father lifts his eyes to the sky and his hat from his head, not without a touch of drama.

"*Omnia mea mecum porto!*" he responds, lifting up his case this time, then dropping it in the dust with pathos.

Eduard Scham, my magnificent father, was blowing kisses like soap bubbles to us through the air from his perch on top of the coachman's seat. Of course, his lyrical clown's mask—one of his last—failed to amuse his little audience. Basically he was trying to hide the pathos of the moment and, above all, to make fun of Mr. Rhinewine, who was obviously taking this move quite tragically, Pharaonically. Lacking the courage to counter Mr. Rhinewine openly, to laugh right smack in his face (after all, Mr. Rhinewine was giving him a ride in his cart), my father tried, in a discreet way, to humiliate Mr. Rhinewine as best he could. Taking up the role of a wandering actor and carnival clown, he suddenly began making light of the sublime role of Noah's descendants and making spiteful remarks on such subjects of veneration as the Righteous Ones, the Old Testament, and the Elect of God, blasphemously interspersing them with comments on the Styrian horses and the milk output of the cows. He had his derby on his knees, implying by this act that it was his intention to stoop to the level of a mere observer in this mediocre farce, or, perhaps he simply had no way of making his hat—that pathetic diadem, that ready-made crown of thorns—part of this role, a role full of petty malice and devoid of true pathos.

"Don't worry about me," he intoned, half turning in our direction as we trudged along behind the cart. "Don't worry at all, as I said, because Mr. Rhinewine has taken me under the wing of his fraternal generosity and with these Pegasuses"— my father pointed to the bulky Styrian horses—"we shall reach the pyramids safe and sound, guided by the hand of God and by righteousness. With the treasures of the generous Mr. Rhinewine, we shall purchase everlasting life, like the Pharisees or at the very least like Judas, and we shall enter into the realms of immortality triumphantly, like Gilgamesh, bribing the guardians of the pyramid with gold pieces and saturating the cherubim at the gates of eternity with Rhine wine." At this point, my father brings his hand to his lips again and blows a kiss into the air to dispel any possible doubt about the meaning of his words.

Dejected and covered with dust, we begin to lag farther and farther behind the cart. In the distance we hear my father's theatrics, which are turning once more into a magnificent soliloquy thrown in the face of the world. By now we can barely make out his words, which compete with the creaking of the carts and the commotion of the animals in their circus cages, whining painfully, desperately, as they leave the green and sunny pastures that evoke an almost human nostalgia and incredible anxiety, for they have an instinctive foreboding (Biblical experience) of the approach of a grand, apocalyptic deluge. At the border between two farms, where the pained trombones of the calves burst out amidst the barking of the dogs and the quacking of the ducks, my father put his hat back on and bowed his splendid head, unable to maintain to the very end that cheap mask of the observer in the drama of life.

"Poor man," said my mother. "I thought he was going to burst into tears."

The following morning, my mother brought my father's belongings out into the sun and left them there in the courtyard until early evening. What was left of his wardrobe consisted of a shabby, greasy riding coat, a black suit that my father disliked and had worn perhaps twice in his life, and a few yellowed celluloid collars. In the evening, she filled the pockets of his riding coat with lavender blossoms and returned everything to the armoire. The sudden change in smells in our room was very hard to take. Accustomed to the ubiquitous, immortal fragrance of his cigarettes, we were struck by the intoxicating, balsamic aroma of the lavender blossoms and the realization that there was something definitive and final in my father's departure this time. The abrupt disappearance of his smell robbed our home of manliness and severity. Its overall interior changed drastically: objects became viscous, corners rounded off, the edges of furniture twisting capriciously until they blossomed into a sort of decadent baroque.

Fifteen days later, my mother and I set out to visit my father. It was a hot summer day. My father was in shirtsleeves. He was fiddling with his suspenders, which slipped down whenever he was not wearing a coat.

"They called me to the Bureau today," he said happily, rubbing his hands. "They put a plus sign behind my name. Schmutz told me. He knows people at the Bureau."

I could hardly recognize him. His departure from our house, and the evaporation of his smell, had left not a speck of doubt as to the finality of his move. I looked upon my own father in disbelief, as if he were outside the perimeter of our lives. Obviously he was aware of this, for he no longer put on an act for us, he did not demonstrate his authority over vital phenomena, he did not show off his erudition, he did not raise his voice to prophetic heights. He was bitterly conscious of the finality of his departure and sensed that we were visiting him as we would an old friend whom we have forgiven everything, that we were making our visit the way people go to the cemetery, once a year, on All Saints' Day.

He lived in a small single room, bare and dark like a monastery cell, in the heart of the ghetto. I understood the situation with bitterness: once fate had allotted him the role of a righteous person and victim and placed him in a hermitage-like setting, my father suddenly grew scared, revised his messianic program, and proved totally incapable of handling matters of a higher order. There was even substantial evidence that he might return to theism. He displayed a remarkable tolerance for his new circumstances, lauding the advantages and comforts of his room and regarding himself as a person on whom destiny has smiled. His capitulation, his acceptance of fate, and his wish to return home had degraded him: he looked like a youthful trainee for the rabbinate. I couldn't wait to get home and forget the sight.

Sensing our impatience and disillusionment, my father said:

"Go home. I'll follow shortly. On the four-forty-five. If that's my destiny."

The courtyard smelled of rancid goose fat and resin. The inside of the fence was unpainted, and resin was oozing from the fresh fir planks. Only here and there, on the connecting planks, had blotches of green paint seeped through. Elderly bearded men pottered about the courtyard, looking like Old Testament prophets, bisecting the circle of the courtyard with cabalistic paths, and when they crossed paths, they would raise their heads to greet each other with a divine glance of forgiveness. Women popped their heads out of windows, their thick dark hair uncombed, their arms strong, to take down or hang up diapers with mysterious haste on that sun-filled day.

On our way out, we caught sight of a boy leaning against the fence. He wore black velvet pants that reached below his knees. He held his arms outstretched at shoulder level, palms out. Other boys, tall boys with sad and serious faces, stood five or six paces in front of him. They said nothing, just stood in a circle like seminarians. Then I saw them move apart and a knife flash and penetrate the fresh fir wood, quivering alongside the boy's shoulder.

After that get-together we didn't hear from my father for a

long time. No doubt, he wanted to overcome the disagreeable impression he had made on us, to redeem the consequences of his bad behavior and inconsistency. A month or so later he sent us a letter. He had tossed this letter, or rather a fragment of an envelope, from a sealed cattle car with a note asking the finder to send it on to the marked address. In his clear hand, which betrayed no nervousness, he had written in pencil: "My collars are very greasy. That is beginning to get on my nerves. I'll send you my new address so that you can send some more. With fatherly affection and concern for all of you, I am yours, etc."

Then, for a number of years, we didn't hear from him at all; no trace of him. He was ashamed, or else some important affairs prevented him from writing. Whatever the case, I began thinking about him intensely, I wanted to get in touch with him at any cost, because his final letter had totally rehabilitated him in my eyes. There was extraordinary resourcefulness in his letter, in the way he had sent it, which pleased my vanity. Besides, he had shown himself to be consistent, as demonstrated by his attitude toward his collars—a matter comprehensible only to those who knew my father well.

Sometimes two or three years will go by without a word from him, yet in other years he will send word three or four times, at short intervals. Sometimes he comes disguised as a traveling salesman or a West German tourist in riding breeches, pretending not to know a single word of our language. The last time, two years ago, he came as the head of a delegation of former concentration-camp inmates who had survived Auschwitz and Buchenwald. He was supposed to give a speech during the commemorative program. But when I ran into him on the street and began to follow him, he retreated to his hotel and hid at the bar, ordering *café au lait* with whipped cream! We found out that he had married in Germany, but the rumor about amnesia was very likely pure fiction. In any case, he was sitting at the bar, his back to me. At first he pretended not to understand that I was addressing him. But hemmed in by the evidence, he finally spoke up in what must have been a feigned foreign accent:

"On what basis, young fellow, are you asserting that I am your esteemed father? Just what sort of *positive proof* do you have to back up such an assertion?"

There was an angry expression on his face, the expression of someone who has been deeply offended. Yet he didn't dare turn his face to me. Instead, he stared at the cup from which he was sipping his *café au lait*, giving himself away even more. Still, I was able to see that he hadn't changed much after so many years, no matter how hard he tried and no matter what cosmetic effects he used. He was a little heavier, a little bulkier, his golden watch chain, which I couldn't positively describe as fake, hung over his belly.

"Anyway," he continued, "even if what you say is true, young fellow, that is to say, that I am your father, I have a perfect right not to remember. Do you know, young fellow, how many years have passed since then? Twenty years, young fellow, twenty years. So there you are. Doesn't it seem logical to you that a person can forget after so many years? To say nothing of the fact that you cite some inconsequential similarity in gait, in voice, in gestures, as proof of my fatherhood. No, no, you are deceiving yourself, young man. My name is Eduard Kohn, I am from Germany, and I have nothing to do with you, young fellow. I have come to your town to give a speech during a commemorative program, and I shall depart thereafter. . . . Good-by and good night, young fellow."

That was merely one of my father's machinations. I assumed that he would no longer appear after this dangerous game, that he would have no desire to run into me and my accusations again, that he would be more cautious in disguising himself. Less than a year later, however, he played in an international chess tournament as a contender for the championship, and he reappeared in our town, making discreet inquiries about me. He published books under a pseudonym, thus sacrificing his ambitiousness, and in his memoirs he heavily retouched the images of my mother, my sister, and myself and spoke of himself with caution, leaving his readers deprived of autobiographical details. He had become taciturn and suspicious, avoiding interviews and provocations. If he thought that he had been led into a trap, he would resort to the most undignified methods to spare himself my inquisitiveness. One time, he locked himself inside the bathroom at his hotel and stayed there till dawn. I called the desk clerk, fearing the worst, but by the time we had broken down the door with hatchets my father had vanished. The suspicion that he might have squeezed through the plumbing was absurd, yet I offered it with certainty. The more he hid from me, the more determined I was to find him, to rip away the veil of mystery, firmly convinced that I would eventually succeed or, at least, discourage his provocative behavior. If my father had agreed to withdraw nicely from the world, to reconcile himself to death, to commit himself definitively to one world, one country, one family, I would not have created a problem for him. But he continued to vent his spite toward the world, to reject a reconciliation with old age and death, to assume the visage of the Wandering Jew and descend upon me—usually dressed as a German tourist—to provoke me, to torment me in my dreams, to remind me of his presence. If he wanted to demonstrate to us that he was not dead in spite of everything, in spite of the world, which had allegedly wished death on him—all right, fine, I believe him. Why, then, did he want to discredit my aunt Rebecca and her story that he had perished in a death camp, presumably unfit for immortality.

The last time I saw him, he was wearing a black ribbon around his sleeve. He sat, surrounded by drunkards, explaining vigorously to them that he was wearing the band in mourning for himself, since there was no one else to mourn him. This sense of paradox, this black humor that so enraged me, was always there, as was his desire to demonstrate his presence by material proof, by pounding his chest to show that he was alive *in spite of everything*. Presumably aware that I was eavesdropping, he began complaining of pains in the small of his back, feeling his sides with his fingers. Of course, he did not hesitate to relate certain intimate details that were of no interest to anyone outside our family: his own son had once beaten him with his cane. Naturally, he didn't mention that he was dead drunk at the time or that I had struck him on the back with his cane because he had been mistreating my mother, threatening her with the iron tip of his cane. But what irritated me most was his play-acting, his pretense. More than twenty years had passed since I had hit him (I was then seven), yet he was grimacing in front of his audience as if it had just happened. As soon as I came close, of course, he switched to German and pretended to be asking the price of hotel services.

WHO IS THIS MAN AND WHAT DOES HE WANT FROM ME?

I n those ancient, mythical times when men still wore derbies and when the extravagances of Viennese fashion—the late baroque of a decadence obvious even then—reigned supreme over Europe, in a mythical era much older in our minds than in reality and therefore undefined historically, a man wearing a stiff-brimmed black hat, a dark suit, and steel-rimmed spectacles stepped into the Golden Lion café one gloomy autumn day. His ash-gray hair was parted down the middle, in the fashion of the time; his long, bony fingers resembled those of neurasthenics or tubercular patients; his black tie was tied in a thick knot under his high celluloid collar. That high celluloid collar, which became fashionable evidently out of a yearning for those times that were already turning into the remote reality of corrupt semifeudal Europe, which was the crown of Franz Josef's Junker uniforms, imparted exceptional dignity to the body and imposed discipline, held the head proudly, idealistically elevated above eye level, above the world and time. This starched bastard offspring of the Roman collar and military dress, which rounded out men's severe dark suits with its dazzling whiteness, pinched the neck like a yoke and held the line in opposition to the unconstrained casual fashion imported from the New World, this high collar was a token of loyalty to the continental, central European spirit and European bourgeois tradition.

The man paused for a moment in the middle of the entranceway, looking around him indecisively. Just when you might have thought he was going to leave, and when indeed he himself thought so, he suddenly went over to the coat rack and hung up his hat and black topcoat. He went through these motions with such assurance that you would have thought that was what he wanted to do all along. For an instant you would forget that you had just witnessed a scene of great indecisiveness and indifference. With a little more perceptiveness, however, you would realize that you were confronted with a man who didn't know what to do with himself, whose decisions and movements were controlled by obscure mechanisms, by chance. He shot a quick, all-inclusive glance at the other patrons, as if testing the consequences of his sudden decision, as if establishing the co-ordinates of time and space, then he headed for an unoccupied table, the only unoccupied table at the Golden Lion that evening, and sat down stiffly, in an aura of philosophical tranquillity, in semiprofile toward the audience. He took a cigarette from his silver case—snapping a cigarette case open or shut was a fashionable affectation in important conversations, or in exciting, tense pauses in the conversation, or on the verge of a grand, fateful decision— and once he had lit his cigarette he looked as if he had finally gotten his bearings, that he had—in philosophical terms —committed himself, opted for something. The Golden Lion was full of civil servants and single people eating their suppers and drinking their schnapps, but the chatter about municipal taxes and the piquant details of women's fashions had given way to serious talk about the international economic crisis and the Saint Vitus's Day Constitution. Spies and provocateurs had already appeared in the provinces, disguised as working-class leaders with false mustaches, and they were eavesdropping on table talk in the cafés, filling their notebooks with coded markings in tiny handwriting concerning the sus-

123

picious, anarchistic statements made by bourgeois progressives, printers, and bricklayers.

The waiters are replacing the plain white tablecloths with fringed, checkered ones. The taste of goulash, beer, and floor wax is in the air, along with cigarette smoke. The celesta is being tuned. Someone runs his fingernail along the strings, which echo with a crystalline pianissimo like the buzzing of a fly in a glass. Ping-ping-ping. A waiter approaches the man's table, clicks his heels, and bows slightly, waiting for the patron's order with an expression that stops halfway between servility and derision. The waiter hugs a napkin under his arm, holding it with his parasitical white hand. Then he turns abruptly and goes off, returning shortly with a glass, which he places in front of the customer as if it were some extraordinary thing, an orange or a coconut. The strings of the celesta reverberate softly, like a buzzing fly.

The man drains his glass of schnapps, bending from the waist, somehow bending his whole body. Then he puts the glass back down on the table like an empty cartridge.

And now, in addition to the physical description, which is guaranteed to bear a resemblance to the original and is based on contemporary photographs and sketches, here is the rest of what we know about this man, everything that we have learned about him in the course of long years of effort and reflection, here are the results of our investigations, of a twenty-year survey conducted among his friends and acquaintances, among close and distant relatives, in police stations and ministries, here—in a word—is the sum total of all our uncertain knowledge about him, based likewise on his personal documents, certificates, diplomas, fingerprints, personal correspondence (at least the small part of it that reached our hands considerably later), judicial verdicts, and medical and military reports, based also on the legend passed down by these contemporaries of his who are still among the living, the sort of legend that entwines itself around every human being, based on palmistry, telepathy, and the interpretation of dreams, here is *everything* we know about this man prior to his fateful (let us repeat: "fateful") arrival at the Golden Lion café.

Eduard Scham, for this man is none other than he, the mysterious Father, suddenly appears in that café on that murky autumn evening in 1930, surfacing out of anonymous millions, isolating himself from the total and chaotic darkness of the world, *in medias res* taken rather too literally, like a Book of Genesis that falls open somewhere in the middle while the first part is illegible or lost. About his parents: we were able to find out only their names, which are meaningless in themselves except that they open up two peepholes for the researcher's wild imagination. His father's name was Mat, his mother's Regina. Regina. What a regal name: Regina! His father had a harelip, if we are to believe a woman who was all too old when she reported this detail to us. But why cast doubt on all our research? Let's have confidence in our witnesses and state that the man with the harelip owned a six-horse carriage (according to the same source), went hunting, and acquired considerable property by dealing in goose feathers. Everything else about that man is wrapped in mystery. However, we are in a position to confirm the accuracy of the report about the carriage, by virtue of our discovery—after the passage of so many years—of the stables where the carriage horses had been kept. By the time we were able to verify the existence of the stables, which is to say, after we arrived in the village where my father's relatives lived, the stables had been turned into a woodshed, but when the earth was dug up for our relatives to bury their valuables, the deeper layers of the soil still stank of horse urine—a fact that corroborates our theory that smells are everlasting, a theory that is quite daring but that has been confirmed on many occasions. We visualize the man with the harelip as an eccentric, a decadent offshoot of a once-powerful tribe that degenerated following the move from its original homeland to the shores of the New World. From that harelip, as from the fossil wing of a prehistoric bird, we infer the overall appearance of the species, climatic conditions and cataclysms. In the absence of sufficient evidence, however, we withdraw in utter disillusionment, we relinquish our quest in the face of the temptations opened up by our bold hypotheses.

Eduard Scham's childhood is no less ambiguous. It was a bucolic childhood spent in a conservative society in the shadow of the six-horse carriage, profits from moneylending, and double-entry bookkeeping. Can you imagine an Eduard Scham, clairvoyant and oracle, dressed in short pants, watching horses mate on his father's property? How do you picture the moment that marks the urbanization of Eduard Scham, during his commercial studies in Zalaegerszeg? Or the historic moment when he first put his elongated neck inside a stiff white celluloid collar as into a yoke, thereby gaining a symbolic entry into the strict ranks of European freethinkers? How do you conceive of his revolutionary, historically far-reaching decision to break with his parents, with his numerous sisters, with his brother, with his name? How do you conceive of the history of his illness, how do you conceive of the origins of that godlike rage in him, the rage that would result in his renunciation of his share of his father's inheritance, in his preposterous decision to declare a crusade against the whole world, gods, religions, in his deranged idea of subjugating the world through renunciation and philosophizing? And how do you envisage this genius, this theoretician of revolution, this prophet in his early role of part owner of a brush factory that would go down someday in resounding bankruptcy? How do you imagine him in the role of the young anarchist and saboteur (wearing steel-rimmed spectacles like Russian revolutionary intellectuals) roaming the wide reaches of the Austro-Hungarian monarchy?

Finally, can you grasp the utilitarian idea of his *Urfaust*, which he had begun writing around that time, his first *Bus, Ship, Rail, and Air Travel Guide*, the one that still lacked notations of international routes, the one that was still without a trace of morbid overstatement and mental derangement?

As Eduard Scham downs his fourth or fifth glass of schnapps and puffs away at his ever-present Symphonia cigarette (the tablecloths are stained, wine is flowing, crushed toothpicks float in pools of beer under the tables, gypsy musicians play Strauss and Liszt, conversation and laughter grow indistinct like the underside of a Persian carpet, glasses and silverware jingle behind the bar like triangles, and the round paper coasters under the beer glasses sop up liquid and expand before splitting into thin micalike sheets), let's relate our hero's romantic adventures (we may call him "our hero," for he was not yet our father at the time), let's tell the story as best we can, as we have heard it, aware every step of the way that we'll never find out the whole truth, that we'll have to fall back now and then on the recollections of unreliable witnesses.

What is coming, then, is an extremely hypothetical chapter, a pale reflection, a cheap copy of the grand and passionate love story that talented gossipmongers had spun, the love story that had spread like fire through the secret channels of *petit bourgeois* intrigue, with rich merchants' wives and their daughters over eighteen as participants, sold under the bakery counters, loaves of warm, sweet-smelling bread wrapped up in its passionate pages, and then these galley proofs—the ink still wet—were read on the sly like subversive literature and passed on in the shopping baskets of housewives and servants from respectable homes, eventually provoking attacks of hysteria in spinsters and bigoted widows.

We are also aware that we shall have to disappoint devotees of romantic novels, admirers of unambiguous intrigue and classical tragedy. Indeed, unwilling to depart from reality and the facts, unwilling to betray our own truth, we must acknowledge that we are not in a position to state the basic fact with any certainty: was our hero in love with the mother or with the daughter? I regret to say that this romantic novel, passed on by word of mouth, has long since worn thin as a pink lollipop. Ingenious feminine intrigue, which we consider to be the keeper of history and the creator of myths, asserts paradoxically that he was in love with both, making, as it were, a metaphorical statement about the impossibility of arriving at fundamental truths. Experienced and by no means naïve, feminine intrigue opens wide the gates of Possibility, never providing definitive answers, always preserving its philosophical noncommitment. Feminine intrigue toys adroitly with the serious theory of romantic relativity, quoting numerous possibilities for us—to mention but a few: he was in love only with the daughter, because the daughter was as warm and sweet-smelling as fresh bread; he was in love with the mother, because the mother was well developed, and pliant as dough on a kneading board; he was half in love with the mother, half with the daughter (fragrant abundance); he was in love first with the mother, but then when the daughter grew up (and was counting on half of her mother's bakery plus interest charges for her dowry) he was in love with the daughter—without, however, being unfaithful to the mother; or he was only in love with the daughter but then changed his mind, because the daughter proved to be a silly goose who didn't know how to keep a romantic secret, so he naturally fell in love with the mother again; and finally, in order to end this game with the serious theory of probability, and because the gates of Possibility are open wide and are dangerously tempting, and since the facts don't deprive us of the satisfaction of toying with fate the way it toys with us, let's mention one other possibility, the simplest: he was in love with neither the mother nor the daughter. But we mustn't overdo it! Let's not cast doubt on everything! Isn't the myth of Mr. Scham's love for the daughter or the mother, for Miss Horgos or Mrs. Horgos, the widow, just as real for example as the myth of Tristan and Isolde?

And here is the continuation of that myth.

Monsieur Scham, the sad Tristan, was the victim of a mythic shipwreck. He ran his craft aground on the dangerous sandbars of Mrs. Horgos, the baker's widow, or else of Miss Horgos, who smelled of fresh bread. Monsieur Scham was unable to reduce this disaster, as was his wont, to the level of a commonplace philosophical conclusion about the world's devious ways and the necessity for universal revolution. Instead he resolved to punish the guilty with a cruel penalty, a penalty instructive for mankind.

Such was the beginning of a renowned undertaking, a project of unprecedented dimensions. Monsieur Scham poured every bit of his genius, all his savings, all the hurt of his affront into his campaign. An enormous, loud banner was soon fluttering downtown, on Saint Sava Street, the pole extending from one side of the street to the other, decorated with big red letters and splotched with paint like the tablecloth from a bloodstained feast of the gods. This Chinese dragon that interfered with traffic and touched the streetcar cables, this masterwork of commercial resourcefulness and publicity that was the envy of all the shopkeepers and bakers and that caused panic among small craftsmen and a general decline in bakery and grain shares on the stock exchange, displayed the enigmatic name of the firm and hovered ominously above the sky of the *petite bourgeoisie*, having appeared suddenly and unexpectedly like a comet:

KOHN & CO.
The First Modern Bakery
IN CENTRAL EUROPE
AND THE BALKANS

For days, the newspapers were crammed with articles about this revolutionary enterprise, while private detectives hired by shopkeepers and craftsmen joined crowds of newspapermen in investigating the case and tracking down the identity of the mysterious stockholder hiding behind the name of Kohn and Company. Every day the police received anonymous denunciations, while dozens of fortune hunters and vagabonds of one kind or another claimed to be the force behind the company name, yet they always turned out to be frauds. The city mental hospital admitted several of its own bakery magnates calling themselves Kohn and Company, including—this was the strangest part of all—a number of latter-day Napoleons, who were thus betraying the security and fame of their appellation for the momentary allure of money, riches, and insecurity. A young girl from a respectable home—that was the culmination of the scandal—who had become pregnant by some fortune hunter insisted that the father of her child was that same mysterious, wealthy individual, who she said had revealed his secret in a moment of lyrical passion. But don't think that the steam bakery of Kohn and Company was just a simple-minded swindle. The mysterious businessman's papers, on file with the Chamber of Commerce, were entirely in order, and his accounts, kept on deposit at the First Serbian-American Bank—although maintained in commercial secrecy (which leaked)—bespoke a substantial amount of capital.

Mrs. Horgos was perhaps the only person familiar with the

identity of the unknown stockholder, but she kept the secret to herself, at least at the beginning. The very fact that the big sign was right across the street from her bakery supported the theory that none other than Monsieur Eduard Scham was hiding behind the name of Kohn and Company and that the whole project was aimed at forcing the proud baker's widow —Mrs. (or Miss) Horgos—to her knees. Naturally, the esteemed Monsieur Scham was not disconcerted by the fact that along with Mrs. Horgos he would be forcing into bankruptcy half of the poor shopkeepers and grain dealers of central Europe and the Balkans, that hundreds, perhaps thousands of apprentices would be stranded without jobs and would descend into poverty. What did it matter to him that they would be ignominiously abandoning the revolutionary proletariat to join the classless lumpenproletariat? A lot he cared about all that!

At a public meeting of bakers and stockholders, a meeting that was to approve prompt steps to be taken against the danger menacing handicraft production by the sudden influx of foreign capital and machinery, Mrs. Horgos was the only one to maintain her composure amidst the general panic, stating confidently that the firm of Kohn and Company was a trial balloon that would bounce over the town for another month or so, like a phantom, but that would eventually explode and vanish into thin air.

Her prophecies were soon realized.

Monsieur Scham, magnate and capitalist, bankrupt in love and stockholder in sentiment, stood in the rain amidst a crowd of children, watching sorrowfully as the workmen pulled his sign down from the cable, dropping it in the mud like a defeated standard, while the mob of lumpenproletariat and shopkeepers' sons chanted "God Save the Czar." Unable to watch the frightful spectacle any longer, he walked off de-

131

jectedly, like a wet dog, and spent three days and three nights drinking in a nearby café, demonstrating for the general amusement of the patrons and the waiters that he was indeed the famous bankrupt businessman written up on the front pages of all the newspapers. With his gift for extravagance, for exaggerations of all kinds, he succeeded in three days (and three nights) in turning the remaining capital of the Kohn and Company Steam Bakery into worthless petty cash, which disappeared into the pockets of waiters or fluttered on the bow of the lead fiddler in the gypsy orchestra.

Mr. Scham was sitting up straight, his body numb, until a warm wave of alcohol swept over him, making him feel closer to his own body. This warm rumbling in his intestines, this invisible sun that lit him up inside, restored his personality, and he once more saw his fingers on the table as part of *his own* hand, *his own* body, he had regained his integrity, his body reconstituted and stretched out to its true size, unfragmented, from the tips of his toes to the last hair on his head. He looked around the café with satisfaction, sure of himself, almost powerful, regaining his selfishness, which was now spilling out in all directions like a fluid, but was in no danger of draining off and leaving him in the lurch. He ascribed this fantastic surge of strength to alcohol alone, yet at the same time he felt a shudder akin to fear: some unknown force was welling up inside him. He was afraid that this internal surge of strength would tear him to shreds, this sudden consolidation of his personality, which was taking on a new dimension, a spiritual dimension, and which gave his skin, his flesh, his bones a new sensation: he felt them painlessly, naturally, as if he were a child. From the day he went bankrupt both in love and in business, from the moment he began abusing his body and felt it as something strange, this was the first time—

that evening at the Golden Lion—that he had gathered together the totality of his organs, heart, head, intestines, extremities, and felt them to be close, as if reborn. The silver cigarette case that he held in his hand resumed its dimensions, reacquired its original meaning outside the confines of commonplace utilitarianism, while the celluloid collar was again reduced to the level of a stoic, philosophic accessory to be worn without grumbling and as a matter of pride, like a badge of caste, a spiritual distinction. For an instant he caught sight of his body, dressed and naked at the same time, he felt the hardness of his toenails inside his socks, he felt his skin, white and freckled like a trout, he felt his ashen hair, which crept under his stiff collar and rubbed against the edge when he turned his head. In that one single glance of satisfaction and fresh courage, he saw that everything was there, the same as before: the big, sharp shoulder blades that made him seem a little hunched, the bony joints of his wrists and fingers, everything, absolutely everything, as if they had never been estranged from him, as if he had never hated them. He felt his bottom going numb on the chair, or, to be exact, "that on which one sits," since he had no bottom—his legs grew directly from his hips, like the branches of a compass, to which he ascribed his chronic hemorrhoids, on which he could now reflect without disgust, as if they were a little joke played on him by the gods. Nor did he overlook his penis resting between his legs, that masculine machinery enveloped in a forest of fuzz; rather than regard it with his customary revulsion toward his own body and toward this tormenting, hard masculinity, his glance embraced it remorsefully. Without asking why or how, he had come to accept his body in its entirety and without despair: his suicidal crises were over. . . .

That same evening, at the next table, Eduard Scham spotted a woman, an extraordinarily beautiful woman, and declared quite lucidly, as if wishing to preserve this newly acquired integrity of mind and body (which he rightly associated with the presence of that woman):

"Gentlemen, et cetera, et cetera, et cetera, et cetera, et cetera."

The intense silence that seized the next table for a moment marked the fateful encounter of two creatures, two stars.

The only sound was the snapping of cigarette cases by the men at the next table.

My father left at the end of July, our relatives shortly thereafter, in August. Uncle Otto was the last to go. He personally closed the shutters and the shop door. The double shop door, pasted with colorful enamel signs, always stood open, making the front of our relatives' house look like the wings of a brightly colored bird. But now that Uncle Otto had shut it, the house suddenly turned blind and gloomy. A seal of red wax was affixed to the door, in the cracks where the outer shutters were hooked together, and the door turned into a big gray official envelope containing boring confidential documents. Uncle Otto looked at the seal with satisfaction and then mounted his bicycle to follow the fiacre carrying my aunts Nettie and Rebecca.

My mother continued to water the geraniums on their porch until the first frost of autumn made the blossoms fade and wither away. Dingo, their dog, howled in the night, an ominous, pained howl. He was unaccustomed to the utter silence that now reigned in our courtyard and in the house, which no longer echoed with my father's fearsome basso, or Rebecca's expressions of petty spitefulness—Rebecca, to whom my father was as allergic as to military uniforms or nettles.

The sudden misfortune that had befallen our relatives, combined with the autumnal gloom, brought Dingo and me closer together. For two days after Uncle Otto left, Dingo continued to lie on the terrace, driven by some pathetic ethical norms that didn't allow him to display his unfaithfulness in any crude way, or, like some peasant mutt, guided only by submissiveness and the laws of the belly. So Dingo lay there on the terrace for two days and two nights, whimpering and howling as if he were in a graveyard. One morning we found him in front of our door, still sad but with a clear conscience. In any case, one should not judge him severely. Dingo had always had two masters: the family and me. He was attached to them out of self-interest, if you will, and because of ownership (they had bought him and kept him fed, they took him to be vaccinated against smallpox, or whatever). He was attached to me in an intimate way, through the heart, out of affinity, indentifying with me from the very beginning, *similis simili gaudet:* we were equally lazy and wild at the same, we loved fantasy and play, we were both wanderers and freethinkers by choice.

Dingo and I were friends from the moment the family brought him home, over a year ago. By that time, I had read many books, which I believed with childish innocence. So I knew the stories of numerous foundlings who had begun their hard lives in front of the gates of elegant and noble lords, and in my dreams I saw myself as a wealthy and lofty Spanish prince. I awoke that autumn morning from a proud dream in which I was about to start on a noble campaign to rescue a foundling weeping in front of the baroque gates of my sleep. On this occasion, however, the weeping of the foundling whose fate was in my hands continued beyond the confines of my dream, spreading out, leaking like water, like the urine of a child who has had a wet dream, whose soaking sheets bear witness to the fact that a dream begun in the school toilet has unfortunately overstepped its God-given boundaries. I was clearly awake, wide-eyed as I stared into the milky sky of daybreak, but the crying went on.

This splendid foundling left in front of our door, born out of my dream as if out of a mother's womb, was lying on his side on a pile of rags, looking at me with his bleary eyes like two blue grapes, and licking my palm with his warm pink tongue. His hair was like a desert fox's or baby marten's, shiny and soft, and he had the magnificent miniature paws of a bloodthirsty lion, like five bird beaks peeking out of as many soft pink nests. And his tail, parasitical little thing, went on living its parasitical little life, completely autonomous, full of surprising and unpredictable motions, playful, frisky. Only his head was sad, old before his time, his snout wrinkled as if holding back tears. It was love at fight sight for the two of us. The funniest thing about this puppy was his extraordinary resemblance to old Mrs. Kniper, the village midwife, in the expression of the eyes and in the wrinkles around the mouth. I tried hard to shake off this sacrilegious comparison, but in vain: the puppy had Mrs. Kniper's wrinkled face, always on the verge of tears. The reader should not presume that this comparison is devoid of ulterior motives and ulterior thoughts in my mind. Quite the contrary: a long time ago I heard my mother and Rosica, the laundress, talking about a lady in Novi Sad who had given birth to a litter of six puppies, the product of a sinful liaison with a half-breed German shepherd, to whom she bequeathed her entire wealth while she was still alive. I had taken this story with a grain of salt, of course, but now looking at the puppy in front of our door, I was suddenly quite sure that those stories had not been Rosica's fabrications and that my mother had failed to counter these intrigues not because she didn't want to bicker with this simple-minded washerwoman but because she herself believed in the possibility of such a liaison and of such a result.

You can imagine my astonishment when Uncle Andre told me that they had brought the puppy early that morning right from Mrs. Kniper!

To test my suspicion, I asked Uncle Andre, "Don't you think that this puppy bears an incredible resemblance to Mrs. Kniper?" Uncle Andre, Rebecca's son, doubled up with laughter as he examined the puppy's face, holding it between his palms, stretching his soft velvety ears, pink inside like rose petals. Nonetheless, he didn't think my comparison absurd. In fact, everybody agreed that I was right—my sister, my mother, Aunt Rebecca, everybody. Aunt Nettie laughed her toothless laugh, but then lowered her voice and said that one should not blaspheme God. After that, we never again mentioned that fact aloud, we simply elaborated on the sinful comparison, which began, in my mind, at any rate, to border on pornography.

Uncle Andre told me, as if disclosing a solemn secret, that the dog was going to be named Dingo, after the bloodthirsty dogs that rampage across Australia. This resounding, exotic name implies to me the coming adventures, develops in my mind a picture of a wealthy future, full of undertakings verging on circus tricks, on marvels. This tiny life, this moist snout, these trembling paws that open and close like a thorny blossom—all this has now been handed over to me, this tender plaything of today that would eventually become a dangerous weapon in my hands, a terror to my enemies, guardian of my sleep and my body, yet also a circus attraction standing on its hind legs and smoking a pipe! I suddenly understand, with a great sense of joy, that Dingo is going to belong to me through affinity and the logic of the heart—children are closer to him, in temperament and in their readiness for play and sacrifice. Even if Uncle Andre trains him, teaches him "various skills and tricks," that would be for my good. Uncle Andre will teach him to walk on his hind legs, to smoke a pipe, not to accept food from anyone, but I will teach him to talk. Why shouldn't a smart young puppy, who stares and whines like a person, learn to speak? Not like a stupid parrot who repeats senseless incoherent words incomprehensible even to himself, but like a person, like a child, he would be able to express a whole range of feelings, as diverse and abundant as those he now expresses with his eyes alone.

Separated from his mother, who is now surely grieving for him, calling out to him, Dingo cringes before us in primordial fear, trembles and crawls at our feet, although now and then, for a split second, his ancient instinct makes him unsheath his claws and bare his eyeteeth as he gets ready for the attack, his eyes full of wild menace. But this instinct, this dormant bad blood, this call of the wild—all this is submerged in the morass of upbringing and training, and the intended suicidal, all-destroying gape comes to a halt as the white-skinned child's hand nears him in a friendly fashion, and he licks it and retracts his claws, forgetting his original intent.

Dingo gradually forgets his mother too, whining only when he is alone. Lifting his head from a deep sleep or profound meditation, he calls to her. Then he lets his head flop on his paws and tries to remember his dream. The odor of milk poured into the bowl merges with his dream, becomes its continuation, its capstone. Aware of the deception, he nevertheless is reconciled to the substitute and laps up the milk like a cat. Naturally, the smell of tobacco (that is to say, my uncle Andre, who smokes on the sly) is not present. My aunt Rebecca, her oily dark skin heavy with femininity, appears for an instant behind the curtain of warm milky vapors, to remind Dingo still more of his lost mother. Only I squat

139

beside him, I dip his little snout into the milk, I talk baby talk to him to make him remember my voice and regard the milk as a gift from me, milked from me, as it were.

He lies there, dejected and resigned, blinking his bleary eyes, and suddenly becomes aware that it is not milk he misses but something else, something undefined, something vague, like melancholy, like nostalgia for the distant and the lost. Full of food yet dejected, he casts a disillusioned glance around him, and then tries to seek refuge from his fate in blissful sleep and in a dream in which something remains of his heroic, wolfish ancestors, some atavistic power on which he can sharpen his teeth like a grindstone, a dream in which he is mighty and fearless. At that point, half-asleep, between stupor and a pink glow, he notices his tail, that snake that curls around him, scratches him on the back and sides, seeks a spot to plant a lethal bite. He bristles from atavistic fear and rage, and a grotesque game begins, a furious rondo, a merry-go-round. Sometimes he almost catches hold of the tail, and just as he has decided to settle accounts with it once and for all, the sly creature slips away and begins going in a circle, right in front of his snout.

But that is merely a passing episode that will conclude in a few days with a nonaggression pact, with an eternal alliance, and everything will soon fade into oblivion, overshadowed by the more pungent encounters with fleas, insects, cats, and birds, by a wave of new smells from kitchen, terrace, and courtyard, by the leftovers and garbage, by the fundamental, primordial saga of the gnawed bone. Ordinarily unresourceful and mistrustful, Dingo had discovered an ancient, Biblical truth in his initial contact with a gnawed bone. His first olfactory contact with a rib of beef drew out of him a distinctly unchildlike sound, a muffled, throaty roar that erupted from his very depths, while the contact between his eyeteeth and this somewhat bloody bone coated the soft, tame blueness of his eyes with a wild, savage patina: that bone stood like a bridge between his atavistic prehistory and his present life in the company of bipeds.

For a long time my father pretended not to notice the puppy in our courtyard. The fact of the matter, however, was this: my father was afraid that this little creature would imperil his glory, overshadow him, push him into the background, because for several days the talk was indeed of nothing but the dog, both in our house and at our relatives'. At any rate, this was our relatives' interpretation of my father's attitude of regal indifference. We supported this theory enthusiastically, to discourage our relatives from figuring out the real truth (which need not exclude the rationale for their own version): in his first contact with Dingo, with an unchristened and dumb Dingo, so to speak, my father had suffered a severe shock, which might have had much more tragic consequences. This episode took place in my father's most glorious days, his era of grand spectacles and frenetic bursts of applause in the cafés for his famous performances and lectures, his impromptu singing and Meistersinger improvisations. One overcast autumn morning, he was returning from a two-week swing around the district, pale, eyes partly closed, intoxicated with glory and alcohol, beaten up and humiliated, dressed in a muddy riding coat and smashed derby. All night long he had wandered across the farms, having lost track of which way was north, because the stars were hidden by thick clouds. Stubbornly determined to find his way with the help of the moss on the trees and such methods, he kept on roaming, trudging through mud, falling into trenches, stumbling against fences. That was a hellish night, a night of violent storm, a night full of thunder and lightning, a pitch-black night that foretold his own end and the end of the universe. But his metaphysical fear, his fear of lightning,

141

was nothing compared with the terror that struck him when rabid village dogs came at him, whole packs of dogs, unruly and famished, picking at his tired body and tormented flesh. Of course, my father (being the encyclopedist, the magus, the psychologist, etc.) was not about to abandon himself to the tender mercies of the village mutts, nor did he resort in defense to his iron-tipped cane. No, sir. Long years of experience and acquaintance with cynology had taught him more effective procedures, absolutely infallible ones: "When a dog attacks you," he once confided to me as he was inculcating me with basic bits of knowledge about life, "don't defend yourself, young fellow, with a stick or your legs, like the gypsies. That not only looks mean but also produces contrary effects in canine psychology, arousing dormant canine instincts for self-defense; to be exact, a person is no longer fighting with a dog or with dogs, but with a pack of famished wolves, as intelligent as they are bloodthirsty. Accordingly, young fellow, remember this once and for all: pay no attention to them at first, don't shrink from their barking, ignore their assault—their barking and howling will never really end, it will last as long as one dog and one person remain on earth. And then, there can be no doubt of it, 'man's best friend' will destroy the last representative of the bipeds, will tear him into little pieces, thus concluding the struggle, avenging enslavement, the shameful slavery to man that has lasted for thousands of years, like the bondage of the children of Israel. So much for the history of these relationships. And what conclusion ought we to draw from this, young fellow? One should abominate them and fight them with intelligence, with tricks, that's what. When a pack of rabid dogs heads in your direction, or rather—I mean to say—at a person, one should hit the ground suddenly, face the dangerous, bloodthirsty enemy on all fours, look him in the eye, even bark at him. If a person is wearing a soft hat or derby, he should

142

remove it and place it in front of him. This method, young fellow, has been tested in practice, *in my very own experience*. It is infallible, extremely efficient. Confronted with a four-legged enemy bigger and stronger than he is, and having witnessed a strange metamorphosis and yet another demonstration of the temporary superiority of man, the animal takes to his heels, his tail between his legs. Man, that two-legged usurper, is able to become a quadruped on a whim, the reverse of which he—the dog—can never succeed in doing, at least not in the way he would wish." Putting these theories to test, my father had been crawling through a number of villages on his hands and knees, barking the whole night at rabid dogs. Crushed by fatigue and lack of sleep, consumed by fear, he found himself in the vicinity of our place, sobered up but incapable of recalling whether that horrible night had been a nightmare or reality or, what seemed to him most likely, the beginning of new attacks of delirium like those of ten years ago, the memory of which now returned to his consciousness and threw him into despair, imbued him with an awareness of his own worthlessness. Having caught sight of a yelping puppy curled up in front of our relatives' house, my father fell on his knees, removed his derby, and yelped back at the dog, trying to hit a high-pitched, pained tone. Fortunately, our relatives witnessed none of this, and my mother led him into the house, pretending not to have grasped the magnitude of his humiliation.

That event formed the basis of my father's relations with Dingo. For two years he ignored the dog's presence completely, and Dingo, remembering the autumn night when my father removed his hat and bowed down to him, tried not to disrupt this relationship. But we know that Dingo respected and loved my father, that he never forgot that sublime, pantheistic gesture, because on the eve of my father's departure, Dingo howled all night long, a horrible, pained howl, sensing the magnitude of the loss and anticipating the silence that would settle on our courtyard like ashes. . . . Dingo jogged along for a time behind the gypsy cart, and then, at one point, he approached my father and looked him straight in the eye, forgiving him all insults. "Look," my father said, pretending not to have noticed the dog before. "*Look, there is no one to accompany Eduard Scham to the grave, to Golgotha. Except for a single wretched dog. A wretched, wise dog*," and here he stretched his hand out, then drew it back quickly, consistent to the end. Or perhaps he knew that he had insulted us.

THE autumn after my father's departure was one of deathly silence, dense and sticky, along with quiet hunger, nostalgic evenings, and village fires. At school, we would be given writing assignments such as "Fire in the Village," exciting pieces of reportage full of remorse and prayer. The girls would choke up with tears thinking about this grand, apocalyptic theme, and the paper before us blazed with a glow, while we were pale and had dark circles under our eyes from a sleepless night.

Hunger had put us into an apathetic trance. For hours we would look out the window at the rain or at the migrating wild ducks and cranes. Their flight, their certainty, their godlike honking reminded us of our father, and we waved to them, the birds of heaven. During the interminable afternoons my sister Anna would put on dresses that she had outgrown and spend hours fixing her long brown hair in front of the mirror, coming up with the most fanciful hairdos, which we sometimes thought exceeded the bounds of propriety. Puckering up, she would rub her lips with red crepe paper, which accentuated her paleness even more. Taking a fashionable pose in front of the mirror, she sticks out her bottom, lets her hair fall over one eye, and laughs, an unhealthy, excited laugh that sends spasms through her body and fills her eyes with tears. Realizing that she has gone too far, and pretending to be frightened, she turns her back on the mirror

145

and departs from its frame with a single step, as if stepping out of the water. Then she takes up her picture postcards again, spreading them out like a fan, arranging them one next to the other like cards in a game of solitaire. What do these false kings and jacks say to her, what does this resonant gamut of colors whisper in her ear—bright red autumn roses, sun-filled landscapes, violet-hued panoramas of distant cities? What does this flamboyant kitsch mean to her, these idyllic and *petit-bourgeois* themes, the bell towers of famous cathedrals, these sentimental couples in old-fashioned fiacres or with tennis rackets in hand, these insipid romantic confessions marked with a heart pierced by an arrow? That will always be a secret. My sister Anna is not one to give herself for long to capricious adolescent daydreaming about a man on a white horse; she locks up her dreams in the dark corners of her dresser, along with her intimate feminine lingerie and wads of white cotton. Before she becomes really obsessed with lyrical motifs and daydreams, she giggles and closes down her fan. Then she begins to make a "jewel box" out of the picture postcards, sewing the edges together with silk thread. Indifferent to the contents of the cards, to those faded, unknown handwritings, she sews up into her box the precious bits of evidence, these papyri that I would attempt to decipher on the sly, quick to identify with the personages who had written them or to whom they had been written. "Dear Maruseta," one postcard began, "my Maruseta, jasmines are cultivated here like peas. All the fields are covered with jasmine," and I was already languishing from love as if I had downed a potion, I was dreaming up a naïve, sentimental story in which I was the protagonist, of course, and where everything smelled of jasmine. . . .

Rummaging through these old, yellowing picture postcards, I find that everything has suddenly become confused, everything is in chaos. Ever since my father vanished from the story, from the novel, everything has come loose, fallen apart. His mighty figure, his authority, even his very name, were sufficient to hold the plot within fixed limits, the story that ferments like grapes in barrels, the story in which fruit slowly rots, trampled underfoot, crushed by the press of memories, weighted down by its own juices and by the sun. And now that the barrel has burst, the wine of the story has spilled out, the soul of the grape, and no divine skill can put it back inside the wineskin, compress it into a short tale, mold it into a glass of crystal. Oh, golden-pink liquid, oh, fairy tale, oh, alcoholic vapor, oh, fate! I don't want to curse God, I don't want to complain about life. So I'll gather together all those picture postcards in a heap, this era full of old-fashioned splendor and romanticism, I'll shuffle my cards, deal them out in a game of solitaire for readers who are fond of solitaire and intoxicating fragrances, of bright colors and vertigo.

Our nostalgic seances (a term coined much later, of course) originated one evening in autumn after my father's departure, almost by chance, in one of my mother's impromptu performances. At first, those evenings didn't have a name, but pagan and unchristened they would repeat themselves out of sequence, sometimes entirely unplanned. Actually they came into being through improvisation, like a poem, before gradually crystallizing and turning into an institution with well-defined aims. Of course, we took special care not to spoil those evenings with rules, so they always kept the charm of freshness, even though they were repeated from autumn to autumn for several years and long since passed the confines of the improvisation from which they derived.

We would always begin from the beginning, as if by chance. The most important prerequisite was my sister's absence. My mother and I tacitly adopted this rule, since Anna was an unsuitable medium for spiritistic seances. In her presence, the round table without the iron nails (symbolically speaking) would not start trembling: Anna's suspiciousness and skepticism toward all idealistic and lyrical phenomena dispersed the mystical fog with which my mother and I had enveloped ourselves.

Once my mother had lit the oil lamp which burned a mixture of lubricant and kerosene, our kitchen would suddenly become the fully legitimate territory of the night. The oil lamp, made out of a tin can, would jiggle and screech like a teapot, drilling like a worm through the hard crust of the night, giving our kitchen a place of honor in the starless night. That oil lamp was the only star shining in those disconsolate nights, the nights when rain shamelessly obliterated such concepts as "up" and "down," uniting heaven and earth by elongated lines, crisscrossing like a child's drawing of an autumn day in gray, ocher, and yellow, with red dots in the corners. On such nights our kitchen turned into a miniature chapel, into an altar on the easternmost point of darkness.

Those evenings grew out of silence, whence all things proceed.

My mother and I would first listen in silence to the story told by the rain in long rhythmical verses without a break, in whole stanzas, sometimes in iambs, sometimes in dactyls, a long epic-lyric poem in the manner of Homer and Mérimée, a poem about witches that lie in ambush behind the chimneys, about a nymph passing by dressed in white, hidden by veils and illuminated by flashes of lightning, about a courageous young hero who rescues her at the last minute, about a swan lake, about gypsies who brandish knives and gather bloody gold pieces out of the mud.

Told and retold from evening to evening and from autumn to autumn, the ballad of the prince charming and the evil nymph kept changing, borne from roof to roof and from window to window, expunged and scattered by the wind, undergoing remarkable metamorphoses, nonetheless preserving in innumerable versions its complicated plot, full of dangerous adventures and love that triumphs in the end. Sometimes, mutilated by the wind and forgetfulness, it would leave blank spaces or a series of dotted lines in· place of verses about love or a description—interwoven with gold—of the emperor's horse, weapons, attire. To be sure, my mother and I didn't always fully understand the language of the original, so we translated some verses freely, guided on occasion solely by the sound of the words, lost in archaisms that no longer meant anything at all or else had a very different meaning now, and when we compared our translations, we would find utterly ridiculous differences, and there must have been mistakes as well. We provided identical translations only of the refrain, in long iambs and with a pause after the fifth syllable. In that refrain, if I remember correctly, the onomatopoeia of the original was retained, full of naïve alliteration, of sibilants and stops. The refrain also spoke of love, of course, of the young prince who races through the storm at night on his dappled horse, carrying on his saddle his pallid nymph, soaked to the skin.

On the evening when all this began, we had had our fill of fairy tales, we were irritable and worn out by hunger. My mother was jealous and worried because I had begun—thanks to this steady fare of storytelling—to interpret some of the verses much too freely, to identify with the princes and kings, other times with the handsome gypsy (when he was given the role of knight and lover), having lost all ethical and religious criteria.

"After all, dear, what does all this lead to?" My mother's question was hurried, as she continued brandishing her knitting needles, which crisscrossed like the swords of Lilliputian knights condemned to fight an everlasting duel over the knitted jacket of a Lilliputian charmer.

Clearly, my mother was frightened by our lyrical excesses. Realizing that I had become all too accustomed to this game of translating the rain into verses before going to sleep, she decided to deflect me from the path of poetic vice and bohemian extravagance and so she began to make up stories of her own, thus resorting herself to the marvelous and dangerous falsehood of poetry. Yet her intentions were honorable: she simply wanted to channel my idealism, to cut it down to normal size, to direct it toward some kind of reality, anything so long as it was not merely a fairy tale. She would then tell me, in a long lyrical monologue, the story of her childhood, spent amidst fig and orange trees, an idealized childhood like those in Biblical stories, because there, as in the Bible, golden-fleeced sheep grazed and donkeys brayed, and the fig was the chosen fruit. My mother tried to counter the fairy tales told by the autumn rains with a legend of her own, fixed in space and time: as proof, she would bring me a map of the world (on a scale of 1:500,000, found among my father's possessions) and point with the tip of her knitting needle to her Arcadia, this sun-drenched Eldorado of her idealized childhood, this illuminated Mount of Olives, this black mountain, this Montenegro. Above all, she wanted to diminish the rain's power and free me of the spell in which it held me with its triplets and quatrains. So my mother lighted up the landscape of her childhood with eternal sunlight and bright summer colors, placing it in a cultivated piece of land, in an oasis between mountain ranges and fields of boulders. Carried away by her own storytelling and by her own mythmaking, she would always return to our genealogy, and not without a touch of pride, she would run across our ancestors in the distant and clouded history of the Middle

Ages, amongst medieval lords and ladies of the court, linking them with the rulers and princes of the republics of Ragusa and Venice as well as with Albanian heroes and usurpers. The family tree, which shone in the pale glow of the oil lamp like drawings on the medieval parchments illuminated with gilt initials, included on its more remote branches knights, ladies-in-waiting, and renowned seafarers who sailed from one end of the world to the other, from Kotor and Constantinople to China and Japan. On one branch, close enough for my mother to call her "your aunt," there was an Amazon (or so at least I imagined her), who had made her contribution to the glory of our clan at the beginning of this century, that is to say, in a recent and altogether unmythical past, by beheading a Turkish tyrant. There was also a famous hero-warrior and writer, a renowned leader, who had taught himself to read and write at the age of fifty so as to be able to add the glory of his pen to the glory of his sword, like the heroes of ancient times. This family tree that my mother was planting in the dense, moist humus of those autumn evenings culminated in my uncles, worldly people in the best sense of the word, men who spoke foreign languages and traveled about Europe tearing down old myths. Of those uncles, one, the best pupil in his class, had been invited to luncheon with the King of Serbia, and following this luncheon he dropped in at the Café Dardanelles where he ordered a plateful of fine Serbian beans costing twenty-five paras (including a slice of bread), thus betraying his pan-European principles.

Each of my mother's tales had its own moral, which she would declaim at the end, following a three-quarter pause, like a distich, or else she would have me state the moral, thus testing both my proclivities and my ethical standards. But my mother's stories were not only about knights and kings, about beautiful gypsies, about the last Abencérage; there was also a fable with a double-edged moral, an Aesopian fable with a moral and lyrical quality that ought not be overlooked. This tale, as I have just said, carried two lessons: the one that proceeded from it logically, and the one that proceeded from my mother's repressed fear that I might give myself entirely to the fantasies and nymph tales of those autumn evenings—my father's example had made clear to her how dangerous such proclivities can be. This tale was about a cow who saw her calf, born to her out of pure maternal love, taken away from her. The story is repeated three times, down to the last detail, and breaks off at the same place each time, always just as tragically: traders come and take away the calf with her doe's eyes, and the cow sheds tears, warm, huge cow's tears, and moos painfully, excruciatingly. After that, the cow becomes sick with grief, and her cow's grief makes her barren. She refuses to take food, and she ceases to give milk. The peasant, seeing that his cow would not survive, especially if she keeps refusing the medicinal herbs, slaughters it. At this point, my mother lowers her voice to a lyrical octave, losing the rhythm of the sentence as if she had lost her breath in agitation.

Do you know the end of this wonderful tale, do you know what happened to the mother cow? They found three long, deep, mortal wounds in her heart, wounds inflicted by a butcher knife—a wound for each calf taken away from her.

And that is the end of the fable about the cow with the wounded heart.

"Do you know, dear, what people used to ask me?" My mother's question returned us from the mythical past of her childhood to historical times—which sometimes bordered on my memory. "They would stop me in the street: 'Forgive me, Madam, what do you rub on your children's skin to make them so white?' I just smile and say that I don't rub anything at all on my children—and so far as food is concerned, I just give you milk, fruit, vegetables, sometimes orange juice.

'Forgive me, Madam, I just can't believe it. . . .' But Andi, for goodness sake, I've told you all that before. So there was this woman who stopped me in Kotor, and she says, 'Excuse me for stopping you in the street, Madam, but I'd like to borrow your pattern books.' 'What pattern books?' I say. Then she asks me whether I dress you according to Viennese or Parisian fashions. So I tell her, 'I beg your pardon, Madam, but what you see on Anna, I cut and sewed myself on my Singer machine, and I thought up the whole thing in my own head, and what you see on Andi, well, I knitted that myself too, and as far as the color is concerned, why is it green, well, Madam, that's because of all colors I love green most of all, green, the color of grass. And believe me, Madam, I would gladly show you my pattern books, but I don't receive any, not from Vienna and not from Paris either.' And she says to me . . . For goodness' sake, dear, I've already told you all of that. Dear God, dear God, you were the handsomest children on Bemova Street, and everybody was asking me what I feed my children to make their cheeks so rosy."

"And now tell me," I would say, "about what the heir to the throne is like, how he is dressed, what he says."

"Oh Andi," my mother says, "I think I've already told you that story. Is it possible that I haven't told you what the heir apparent said? My girlfriends in school told me that a young prince was coming to visit, Italian I think, and indeed he came one day to our school incognito, as the saying goes, but he was dressed like a real prince, as good-looking as a girl, with everything shiny—saber, golden epaulettes—yet his hands were white, aristocratic, delicate. He paused briefly, looked at us, smiled, and went off in the company of the other gentlemen, all in splendor, his spurs jingling down the corridor, which had been decorated for the occasion with roses and lilacs. The next day, Signorina Angelica, an Italian woman who taught us embroidery, called me in and told me that the young prince had asked about me, who I was, where I was from, what kind of home I came from, because I appealed to him. I felt like sinking into the ground from shame. Just imagine, Andi, how beautiful your mother was. . . ."

At such moments, my mother would put aside her knitting and take out a box from the bottom of the dresser, a box containing old, yellowed family photographs and daguerreotypes, the corpus delicti of times past, of the imaginary splendor of her youth and of the glory of our family.

And so, gradually and quite unconsciously, my mother poisoned me with her reminiscences, nurturing in me a passion for old photographs and mementos, for soot and patina. A victim of this sentimental education, I yearned along with her for the days that would never come back, for ethereal journeys and faded landscapes as we stood mute over the yellowed photographs.

This gifted young chap, this *Wunderkind*, this poet and pianist—that must be my late father, Eduard Scham (I said to myself). Eduard Scham, doubly and forever dead. And this is my mother, Maria Scham, at a time when she was not yet my mother. The late Maria Scham. And this is my sister Anna, five or six years ago, when we were still living on the street lined with wild chestnut trees. . . . The late Anna Scham. This boy over here with the tiny bell around his neck, like a little lamb, that is me, the late Andreas Scham. . . . On occasion, my mother would try to offset this all-embracing process of dying out—time, fashion, youth —with a utopian vision of some clouded future, but she was not at her best in such moments. These were futile digressions based on guesswork, and soon, through the brilliant careers of my uncles, her brothers, the story would gradually and inexorably revert to the past as into an abyss, while the yellowed photographs lay strewn about us like faded autumn leaves.

Shaking with laughter, Anna would come in the door, fresh from a walk in the rain, like a good angel of the night. Faced with our trance, she would take offense and make fun of us, making allusions to our father and our nocturnal seances. I was relieved that we were able to break the stiff crust of our grieving silence in such an uncomplicated way. As if caught in the act and put to shame, I would gather the photographs from the floor and stuff them quickly into the box, while my mother would sit up so suddenly that the yarn would fall off her lap and bounce away in the dark, like Angora cats leashed to her knitting basket by varicolored threads, and, invisible out there in the dark, they would continue to bounce against the corners of the room, colliding softly, as if playing a game.

THE proofs against my immortality were mounting up. Particularly on such evenings in autumn, when the temptations would become especially painful, and when the sole consolation was the idea of some unattainable paradise, I would begin to doubt all values. Weakened by prolonged hunger, I would stagger into my bed. I would beseech my mother not to turn off the light and not to leave me alone. Sympathetic, but not without a touch of despair, she would promise to leave the kitchen door ajar so as to let a single ray of light into the room. Once she had kissed me and comforted me, she would withdraw to her corner, where she got to work on her tiresome piecework knitting. Finally comprehending the strength of her arguments and the inevitability of sleep, which I had been resisting, I resolved to carry out one of my diabolical and sinful thoughts: I would conquer the angel of sleep, I would take advantage of this ineluctable and painful relationship for my own blasphemous ends. Over the years, my fear of dreams had grown to such an extent that in the morning, when I woke up, my first thoughts were akin to mortal fear: day was ahead of me, brief day that would end inevitably in the gloomy abyss of sleep, no matter what. The unconscious parallel that I drew in my mind between the cycle of day and night and the cycle of life and death had become utterly unbearable, overshadowing the second part of the comparison as if it were a matter still to be contemplated, whereas the fact of sleep kept on being a presence, a reality, with all its anxieties, all its wonders and temptations. Night after night, for years, I dreamed a dream that repeated itself, with tiny variations: I would be lying in my bed (in my dream) when a dense, ominous silence suddenly set in, a silence full of foreboding. This explosive silence would saturate my bones and my consciousness, giving me a lump in my throat and making me short of breath, because this was only the frightful precursor of what I suspected was on the way. And what was on the way had neither a name nor a shape; it resembled a thunderstorm, an infernal storm-avenger that came like a thief in the night, sneaky—like death —to catch adults and children in their sleep, sneaky. Gloom would descend, a dense Biblical gloom, the divine angel-murderer would fly over the earth, the birds would fall silent, the flies cease buzzing, the leaves stop rustling. That would set the stage for the arrival of the nameless Something that noisily broke down the door to our room, facing me, grabbing for my throat. "Andi! Andi!" I would hear my mother's frightened voice, but it would take me a few moments to realize that this was not my mother's voice calling out to me helplessly in my dream but the blessed end of my nightmare. "You've been sleeping on your left side again, dear," she would whisper as she rested her hand on my forehead. What surprised my mother the most was the same old story every time about the Something approaching me, yet in spite of all my efforts I had never been able to catch sight of that Something. I was in a state of such shock following these nightmares that my mother understood they were not something I could easily describe.

To hold off my nightmares my mother would let me sit next to her in the kitchen for a long time, carrying me off to bed once I fell asleep. Since she was completely indifferent to my choice of reading matter, regarding all books as equally useful in achieving oblivion (she was not wrong), she would allow me on occasion to read late into the night. She had noticed that, thanks to books, I was gradually gathering courage and was beginning to struggle with my nightmares on my own. Novels of adventure, of crime and heroism, helped make my dreams tangible, and I was soon able to make out the face of my attacker under his black mask, the Something that broke down the door to our room like a phantom—surely no small achievement in the evolution of my dreams. Grand and invisible, the vague and unknown Something that had been strangling me with its spectral hands was now shaping into something specific, into a simple-minded thief or a hired murderer of children who was making an assault on my life. Naturally, that was an easier proposition for me to deal with. As I catch sight of him peeking around the corner at me, as we stare at each other like beasts of prey, arriving at a mutual decision as to whether to attack or flee, I suddenly realize that any attempt on my part to attack or to flee would be laughable in this terrifying game. I have no more chance than a rabbit cornered by hunting hounds because fear has bewitched my legs and turned them into lead. I can't budge. Horrified, I make a powerful effort of will and consciousness to talk in my sleep: I am dreaming, I AM DREAMING, and so I trick the murderer and leave him miles behind, and surely my disappearance must have befuddled him and driven him to rage. Of course, I wasn't always successful in bringing off this maneuver. Sometimes, faced with some threat and with my own impotence, I would dream of waking up, but I shifted not into waking life but into some other dream, into another level of my very own dream, a dream sometimes still deeper and more clouded.

By analogy with sleep, the thought of death came to obsess me more and more, to overwhelm my fantasies about the possibility of escape and immortality. This terrible thought was helped along, naturally, by the novels I read, in which shrewd, tough heroes stood before the phenomenon of death and dying like helpless children, firing their guns into the void, knocking their iron fists against death's bony jaw. The final departure of my father, in which I had never wished to believe deep down inside, was one of the experiences that served as a basis for my theory of the impossibility of escape. For I knew that my father would have been able to befuddle death with his eloquence, with his philosophy, with his theories, to discredit it by some extraordinary discovery or device if death were at all susceptible to being discredited at a human level. This frightful awareness did not weaken the intensity of my devoutness, but it made it more hesitant and less warm. At night, as I lay in my bed tossing and turning in a feverish fear of death, which I foolishly equated with death, I would suddenly see my own personality from the standpoint of eternity, *sub specie aeternitatis,* as if illuminated by some cloudy truth, and in terror, I would grow aware of my own nothingness from the vantage point of eternity, which at such moments I saw as the enduring state of the world, in painful counterpoint to my own transience.

My realization of the time and space in which I had placed my anxiety and my ineptness at moments of apocalyptic illumination began to corrode my moral purity and my divine and saintly visions. I began to understand the derangement of my heroes: they had obviously become courageous and fearless in order to counter their own sense of worthlessness. Of course, I barely dared to admit to myself that the idea of power and courage born out of the worthlessness of life (the brevity of life never seemed so clear to me as it did when I'd first encountered it at age nine) fascinated me. After that, even the fates of the heroes suddenly seemed less tragic to me, their long years in prison irrelevant from the standpoint of eternity. Had I not condemned myself to hell (to purgatory at best—an insignificant difference) and realized that there was no place for me in paradise because of my deeds and especially my sinful thoughts, I would have made an effort to gain a place in eternity, but it was too late: doubt was dangerously gnawing away at me.

My heresy was especially strong in my dreams, when the sense of eternity intensified and grew urgent. In my dreams, I covered the same territory as in my waking life, but my consciousness kept a different time from real time, or rather of time outside time. The eternity of the world and the worthlessness of my own life within this enormous passage of time had become obvious, almost palpable. I found the eternity that was denied me in my waking life but dominated me in my dreams, seductive as well as painful. Free of the scruples of everyday morality, *conscious* of my worthlessness, I had no fear of God in my dreams: I wanted compensation for my recent sojourn in hell, I wanted to live my own life, my superlife, in my dreams if not in reality. I had no hope of deceiving my guardian angel, because he was with me and recording reports about my behavior in his notebooks for double-entry bookkeeping, but I consoled myself with the fact that his presence in my dreams had become quite tolerable, his whispering barely audible.

As a result of all these experiences, the terror began to vanish from my dreams. Whenever I shrieked or cried out in my sleep, my mother would find me lying on my left side or on my back, so I made an effort to go to sleep on my *right* side, my knees tucked up to my chin (defense against hunger and winter's cold as well) to enable me to maintain that position for as long as possible. This eventually became a habit. Before going to sleep, I would turn from side to side, but stay on my left long enough to all but doze off, on the left side where my heart was, the source of my nightmares. At the last moment, however, when there was no longer any doubt that sleep was on the way, I would make a final effort of consciousness and flip over to my right side, where only pleasant dreams awaited me: I would be riding Uncle Otto's bicycle, I would be flying in a high arc over the river. . . . The realization that I was able to control my dreams, channel them in a particular direction by my choice of reading matter or by thinking certain thoughts before going to sleep, resulted in an explosion of my darkest impulses. In fact, I was living two lives (not a trace of bookishness in that), one in reality and the other in my dreams, which produced in me an extraordinary and sinful joy. Since we were going hungry at the time, diabolically hungry, hungry to the point of screaming, I would think of food before going to sleep: I would imagine an abundance of the foods for which I was yearning, conjure up their smell with painful accuracy. Usually, however, I lulled myself to sleep with my classic dream: we are on the train, in a first-class compartment, my mother arranges a damask napkin on the folding table and cuts poppy-seed cake, I begin to eat, I taste and smell the poppy seeds, I gather the crumbs from the napkin. But this meal, this ritual, lasts too long, so doubt suddenly creeps in by the side door of the dream, my appetite remains unsatisfied, yet I understand with one tiny fragment of my consciousness that this is just a dream, so I decide that I ought to think up some more cakes and fruit for my banquet and change it all—as Jesus changed the water—into the wine of my dream. At that very moment, that splendid moment of almost godlike lucidity, the thought *I am dreaming this* I AM DREAMING THIS makes its way into my consciousness. I try to reject the thought, not because it is false but because I know that it is true. I wake up with a sensation of monstrous hunger in my entrails, and I twist and turn for a long while, trying to set some other trap for myself.

When I am not eating poppy-seed cake in my dreams, I am meeting, in the brilliant sunshine of our village, on the riverbank, in a field of flowers, Mademoiselle Magdalena, the school principal's housemaid. She is a dark-eyed, buxom girl who had come our way with an army officer from Budapest. He abandoned her, and she became a seductress, the object of rivalry among the village youths. I know for sure that she had fornicated with my young cousins, because I had spied on them, and I often ran into her on that embankment at dusk as she made her way to a secret rendezvous. Once she had even patted me on the head when I stopped to say hello, and I trembled with fear that she might detect my intentions.

The decision I had reached, namely to rape Mademoiselle Magdalena in my dreams, resulted in a complete fiasco. The same sequence recurred in every dream, almost down to the last detail, just as in my waking life: Mademoiselle Magdalena is walking along the embankment and then descending into the field, to pat my head. My shameful decision evaporates as soon as I realize that this is possible only in my dreams (I AM DREAMING, I AM DREAMING). I wake up, full of shame and remorse. For a long time afterward, I would avoid her, I would run away and hide in the shrubs by the river. I was afraid that she might recall my dream, because she had been in it, as real as I, and close enough to have seen my decision written all over my face, my trembling, even the motion of my hand as I reached to grab her breasts.

One night, however, in a meadow, in a meadow under a wild pear tree, I ran into a woman I had never seen before, and I decided to rape her. I was obsessed with the sophistry of my dream, in which I could sin not only without being punished but without committing a sin, because the woman existed only in my dreams, she was alive only to the extent that the young heroines in my evening reading existed, but more anonymous, more abstract. The only advantage of the one in the dream was that she was incarnate—at the level of the dream, of course. She was a peasant woman in her thirties, light-complexioned, on the thin side. She was picking wild pears, and she smiled at me. We were alone. Once I made up my mind I felt relief and pride, though I almost fainted from fear and excitement; the backdrop vanished suddenly, like a miracle, and we stood facing each other, just the two of us, eye to eye. I had time to rejoice in the beauty of my victim, to admire her complexion, her eyes, her shiny teeth. When it occurred to me that she might resist or turn me over to the police, I laughed because I was the one who had created this woman to fulfill my dream, so forward march, lift up her skirt, young fellow, you invented her, I must be dreaming, I MUST BE DREAMING, yet the woman continued passing by and smiling, laughing at my indecision and my fear. My realization that I was dreaming negated my decision and compelled me to accept my dream as something that I could not entirely mold by will power, that I could not exploit as a gold mine of sin and vice.

On another level of that same dream, I was running away, but unable to take off. For a long, long time, I was sinking into an abyss, gently, as if flying, although I knew what was waiting for me down below. I still wanted to enjoy myself for as long as possible, to enjoy the beauty of this dizzying fall, because I knew that I would wake up when I hit the ground, because I knew that none of this was true, I am dreaming, I AM DREAMING, the same as before, I AM DREAMING.

My descent into hell ceases to be gentle at that instant. I know that I am dreaming, and I check which side I am sleeping on.

With a final effort of will, I turn over to my right side: *O, mea culpa, mea maxima culpa*, oh heart, oh night!

Leaning on my elbows, panting like a puppy, I try to shake off visions and sinful thoughts, to forget defeats. In the ashgray morning light, I catch sight of my mother and my sister and—holding my breath—check to make sure they are asleep. Good, they couldn't have witnessed my nightmares, I couldn't have betrayed myself with words or gestures. Eternity and death, the mystery of time, loomed up before me, unattainable and invincible.

In the gloomy cowl of night and morning's semidarkness, time congeals like milk, yet I innocently try to see through it. All I see is the immense silence of worm-eaten objects, things oppressed by their own nocturnal specific weight, the suspended bell-clapper in the heart of things that are weighed down by oblivion, that are practically nonexistent, that have been horribly and mercilessly reduced to specks and surrounded by a violet aureole. The painting on the wall, the guardian angel over our bed, the night tables, the vase yawning empty: all this is now a gigantic, heavy void lacking any proportion, for in the twilight their positions are just barely outlined. Actually, I can only guess their location from a day-old memory that already seems so distant. While I sense the presence of my mother and my sister as life, although I don't hear their breathing, I sense the death of objects in that dark night almost tangibly and as a painful burden, because this is one more proof of the reality of death, and I am beginning to equate my own death with the oblivion into which objects sink overnight, so a tremor of compassion for the destiny of the world comes upon me. The tiny round ticking heart of the clock emerges as my sole consolation, as the sole omen of victory over the void, first as a sound and then as a slight metallic glow, heroic in its resistance to death, night, and time, and I try to raise its victory to the level of a universal triumph, to lodge its ticking heart in night's dead body so as to reanimate it and raise it above its feeling of defeat. I rest my ear on the dead night table and hear it vibrating, hear its artery throbbing beneath its throat like a lizard's, I strain my eyes to make out the far-reaching consequences of this victory, and I seem to see traces of orange color on the wings of the guardian angel, and carried away by phantasms, I blow up this victory into a universal triumph of color and of the daylight that is beginning to stream in from all directions, to leap out of the picture frames, to sprout up in the form of large, flamboyant roses on Anna's dress hanging on the closet door.

With the coming of dawn, conscious of victory and happily surprised by the life that is awakening both in objects and in me, I resume sleeping my true and only sleep, the sleep which knows neither surprises nor defeats.

Collins rushes up to the table, lights the lamp, and brings it closer. Wentworth and Louisa help the mulatto girl sit up. Her eyes were shut, her breathing weaker and weaker. Collins lifts the lamp high over his head and observes the girl. She clasps a tiny ampulla. On her lips, there were several minute grains of powder (Chapter XXXIII). "Wind! Wind!" came the shout from the deck. "At last!" Wentworth thought to himself happily. "At last, the calm is over." That happened one morning, some two weeks after Marcia's death. He was sitting with his girl and Sutherland on the veranda and gazing out at the sea, the great shining sea that had begun here and there to ripple into waves.

I could hear the pounding of the waves against the shores of distant continents, Tahiti, Malaya, Japan. The history of the world stood before me like a blooming rose, an adventure accessible only to the boldest, the great history of the world, one chapter of which had just occurred—the splendid happy ending to a love story. Pearls in shells, mulatto women, coral reefs, coconuts, exotic flora and fauna, all of these were divine effluvia tailored to fit my dreams. I had the ability to conjure up their colors and shapes, and their smells in particular, with such accuracy that seeing the original articles could only have meant downgrading them in my eyes, like a blind man who sees for the first time, in the sense that I had created in my mind only the quintessences of colors, tastes, and smells, I had created ideal specimens of flora and fauna, I had reverted to the experience of my dreams and my Biblical reading, all the way back to Noah. Blessed be the division of the world into the good and the bad! I was lenient with my heroes, forgiving them and favoring their romantic adventures. By the end of a novel my heroes will have survived dangerous undertakings in order to gain heaven's reward in the form of the divine offspring of some mulatto woman with lips like a pomegranate or of some white-skinned girl (with a freckled nose) who would fold her arms around the righteous man's neck like a lily. Overwhelmed by the severity of the Biblical stories, aware of my inability to obey all ten commandments, branded from birth with original sin, disturbed by the catechism that page by page proved to me my sinfulness and my fall and the inevitability of my fall and the certainty of hell, I have become addicted to my novels in the same way that I am addicted to the sinful thoughts that I cannot drive away, the thoughts that are nevertheless less sinful—gauged against the strict, Draconian laws of the Last Judgment—than deeds, acts. But of novels, I grab seas, lands, skies, loves. Oh life, oh world, oh freedom! Oh father of mine!

One autumn evening (let the reader permit us to isolate this event), one ordinary autumn evening when I was eleven years old, without any preparation, without any prior announcement, without any portents in the heavens, Euterpe —muse of lyric poetry—made her astonishingly simple entrance into our house. That was the only big event of the season, the sole bright spot in the status quo of that murky autumn. I was lying on the wooden chest in the kitchen, covered with a blanket, desperately determined to sleep through the autumn tedium and to overcome hunger by stoic meditation on the future, on love. Hunger makes for subtlety, subtlety makes for love, love makes for poetry. My extremely vague idea of love and the future turned into a glittering map of the world outlined in bold colors (a supplement to my father's book), into the unattainable, into despair. To travel! To love! Oh Africa, oh Asia, oh distance, oh life of mine! I blinked my eyes shut. Under the eyelids, shut tight to the point of pain, gray reality collided with the flame of fantasy and flared up in a reddish glow that soon flickered into yellow, into blue, into violet. The heavens opened up for just an instant, the fanfares started up, and I caught sight of bare-bottomed cherubs fluttering about the bright reddish focus of paradise, flapping their wings like flies. But this lasted, as I said, only an instant. Immediately thereafter I began falling dizzily into a deep pit, but this time it was no dream. A marvelous, all-embracing rhythm quivered inside me, and the words came out of my mouth as if I were a medium speaking Hebrew. The words were indeed in some strange language, full of new resonance. Not until the first wave of feverish excitement had passed did I take it upon myself to decipher their meaning. Under the billowing surface of the music and rhythm, I discovered words that were quite ordinary, similar to those in the barcarolles my father used to sing. Entirely conscious of the impossibility of translating these verses faithfully, I beg the reader to take note of the elements they contain, the components from which they evolved, which may prove that they had truly existed in some former time. Here you are: this lyrical and fantastical ballad, this authentic masterwork of inspiration consisted of the following words arranged in an ideal and unrepeatable sequence: *coral reef, instant, eternity,* and *leaf.* Plus a totally incomprehensible and enigmatic word: *plumaseria.*

Panic-stricken, I sat hunched on the chest for a while longer and then told my mother, in a voice cracking with excitement: "I have written a poem."

Where have the glittering picture frames gone from these pages, the violent-painted fiacres, the flowers that wither in their vases? Where have the trains gone, and the hanging baskets that sway on the platforms of provincial railway stations? Where is the bluish light from the first-class train compartments? Where is the lace that flutters like a fan on the green plush seats? Is it possible that the embellishment machine, the crystal vessel through which the current passes in the electroplating process, has come to a halt so soon? Where is the gilt of the antique picture frames, or the smile of the Mona Lisa?

We are witnesses to a great breakdown in values. Due to dampness and sudden changes in temperature, the gilding has peeled off the picture frames, along with the color of the guardian angel's wings and the lips of the Mona Lisa. Our furniture, having been dragged around the railway system as slow freight at the time when my father was playing his role as the Wandering Jew, was scratched and is now falling apart, rotting as if contaminated with phylloxera. Little red bugs, which my mother called by their popular name "American bugs" and my father *Ageronia Mexicana*, have transformed our dressers into wrecked hulks rescued from the sea, bereft of their sheen and riddled with a whole labyrinth of tunnels. From time to time great hunks of wood would break off of their own will, and on the inside we discovered some Indian message in magnificent hieroglyphics that we chose to interpret as a voice from the Other World. My mother's Singer sewing machine, too, vanished in the confusion of war like an orphan, a runaway oversensitive to tremors. That was a heavy blow to all of us, especially my mother. Similar fate befell the other object that our family had once treasured: our ancient couch, the one the color of rotten cherries, disintegrated somewhere along the line between Budapest and Kanjiža. To the very end, however, it never failed to give off its fine sound. According to my father, who had attended the claim commission's inspection, the couch had a resonance that made it sound like a harpsichord. Dampness and greenish-gray mold, the color of decay, now reigned in our house. This misfortune derived from the inability of our kitchen stove to generate a real flame: we lacked a real blaze, there was no glow. This made more of a mess in the house, at the beginning, before we grew accustomed to the smoke. After we had had a good cry we would move through a cloud of bluish-gray smoke as if it were our natural element, and in our spiritualized language we called it our "hearth" and we would cough, choke up, as if smoking some expensive, strong cigars that combined the aroma of evergreens with the idea of a hearth. We fired our stove with dry pine cones that we gathered in the woods in the autumn and carried home in big sacks, like coal. Oh those wonderful ore pits, that gold mine! Oh Count's forest, my father's forest! Dew would be dripping from the trees, and the resin—mixed with the smell of the evergreens—had a prophylactic effect on us and who knows what else. There was joy in our strolls through the woods in autumn. We would be making our way home, weighted down with sacks, and stop at the edge of a thicket to catch our breath and wait for evening to come. Then a hunter's horn would bleat a greeting somewhere in the distance, and a solemn stillness would descend on us.

Our father's ghost hovered in the woods. Didn't we hear him blowing his nose into a scrap of newspaper only a few minutes ago, while the woods reverberated with a triple echo?

"We have to get going," my mother would say at that point. "Lord, how quickly it gets dark here."

SELECTED DALKEY ARCHIVE PAPERBACKS

PIERRE ALBERT-BIROT, *Grabinoulor*.
YUZ ALESHKOVSKY, *Kangaroo*.
FELIPE ALFAU, *Chromos*.
    Locos.
    Sentimental Songs.
IVAN ÂNGELO, *The Celebration*.
ALAN ANSEN, *Contact Highs: Selected Poems 1957-1987*.
DAVID ANTIN, *Talking*.
DJUNA BARNES, *Ladies Almanack*.
    Ryder.
JOHN BARTH, *LETTERS*.
    Sabbatical.
ANDREI BITOV, *Pushkin House*.
LOUIS PAUL BOON, *Chapel Road*.
ROGER BOYLAN, *Killoyle*.
IGNÁCIO DE LOYOLA BRANDÃO, *Zero*.
CHRISTINE BROOKE-ROSE, *Amalgamemnon*.
BRIGID BROPHY, *In Transit*.
GERALD L. BRUNS,
    Modern Poetry and the Idea of Language.
GABRIELLE BURTON, *Heartbreak Hotel*.
MICHEL BUTOR,
    Portrait of the Artist as a Young Ape.
JULIETA CAMPOS, *The Fear of Losing Eurydice*.
ANNE CARSON, *Eros the Bittersweet*.
CAMILO JOSÉ CELA, *The Hive*.
LOUIS-FERDINAND CÉLINE, *Castle to Castle*.
    London Bridge.
    North.
    Rigadoon.
HUGO CHARTERIS, *The Tide Is Right*.
JEROME CHARYN, *The Tar Baby*.
MARC CHOLODENKO, *Mordechai Schamz*.
EMILY HOLMES COLEMAN, *The Shutter of Snow*.
ROBERT COOVER, *A Night at the Movies*.
STANLEY CRAWFORD, *Some Instructions to My Wife*.
ROBERT CREELEY, *Collected Prose*.
RENÉ CREVEL, *Putting My Foot in It*.
RALPH CUSACK, *Cadenza*.
SUSAN DAITCH, *L.C.*
    Storytown.
NIGEL DENNIS, *Cards of Identity*.
PETER DIMOCK,
    A Short Rhetoric for Leaving the Family.
ARIEL DORFMAN, *Konfidenz*.
COLEMAN DOWELL, *The Houses of Children*.
    Island People.
    Too Much Flesh and Jabez.
RIKKI DUCORNET, *The Complete Butcher's Tales*.
    The Fountains of Neptune.
    The Jade Cabinet.
    Phosphor in Dreamland.
    The Stain.
WILLIAM EASTLAKE, *The Bamboo Bed*.
    Castle Keep.
    Lyric of the Circle Heart.
STANLEY ELKIN, *A Bad Man*.
    Boswell: A Modern Comedy.
    Criers and Kibitzers, Kibitzers and Criers.
    The Dick Gibson Show.
    The Franchiser.
    George Mills.
    The MacGuffin.
    The Magic Kingdom.
    Mrs. Ted Bliss.
    The Rabbi of Lud.
    Van Gogh's Room at Arles.
ANNIE ERNAUX, *Cleaned Out*.
LAUREN FAIRBANKS, *Muzzle Thyself*.
    Sister Carrie.
LESLIE A. FIEDLER,
    Love and Death in the American Novel.
FORD MADOX FORD, *The March of Literature*.
CARLOS FUENTES, *Terra Nostra*.
JANICE GALLOWAY, *Foreign Parts*.
    The Trick Is to Keep Breathing.
WILLIAM H. GASS, *The Tunnel*.
    Willie Masters' Lonesome Wife.
ETIENNE GILSON, *The Arts of the Beautiful*.
    Forms and Substances in the Arts.
C. S. GISCOMBE, *Giscome Road*.
    Here.
DOUGLAS GLOVER, *Bad News of the Heart*.
KAREN ELIZABETH GORDON, *The Red Shoes*.
PATRICK GRAINVILLE, *The Cave of Heaven*.
HENRY GREEN, *Blindness*.
    Concluding.
    Doting.
    Nothing.
JIŘÍ GRUŠA, *The Questionnaire*.
JOHN HAWKES, *Whistlejacket*.
AIDAN HIGGINS, *Flotsam and Jetsam*.
ALDOUS HUXLEY, *Antic Hay*.
    Crome Yellow.
    Point Counter Point.
    Those Barren Leaves.
    Time Must Have a Stop.
GERT JONKE, *Geometric Regional Novel*.
JACQUES JOUET, *Mountain R.*
DANILO KIŠ, *Garden, Ashes*.
    A Tomb for Boris Davidovich.
TADEUSZ KONWICKI, *A Minor Apocalypse*.
    The Polish Complex.
ELAINE KRAF, *The Princess of 72nd Street*.
JIM KRUSOE, *Iceland*.
EWA KURYLUK, *Century 21*.
VIOLETTE LEDUC, *La Bâtarde*.
DEBORAH LEVY, *Billy and Girl*.
    Pillow Talk in Europe and Other Places.
JOSÉ LEZAMA LIMA, *Paradiso*.
OSMAN LINS, *Avalovara*.
    The Queen of the Prisons of Greece.
ALF MAC LOCHLAINN, *The Corpus in the Library*.
    Out of Focus.
RON LOEWINSOHN, *Magnetic Field(s)*.
D. KEITH MANO, *Take Five*.
BEN MARCUS, *The Age of Wire and String*.
WALLACE MARKFIELD, *Teitlebaum's Window*.
    To an Early Grave.
DAVID MARKSON, *Reader's Block*.
    Springer's Progress.
    Wittgenstein's Mistress.
CAROLE MASO, *AVA*.

FOR A FULL LIST OF PUBLICATIONS, VISIT:
www.dalkeyarchive.com

SELECTED DALKEY ARCHIVE PAPERBACKS

FOR A FULL LIST OF PUBLICATIONS, VISIT:
www.dalkeyarchive.com

Printed in the USA
CPSIA information can be obtained
at www.ICGtesting.com
JSHW022344140824
68134JS00019B/1674

9 781564 783264